I0732145

Sweet Distraction

by

Neesa Lee

Published by:
Powder River Publishing LLC
1014 Black Mountain Road
Thermopolis, Wyoming 82443

Copyright © 2023
ISBN: 978-1-956881-27-1
Printed in the United States of America

No part of this publication may be reproduced, stored, transmitted in any form — electronic, mechanical, digital photocopy, recording, or other without the express written approval of the author.

All rights reserved solely by the author. The author guarantees all are original and do not infringe upon the legal right of any other person or work. The views expressed in this book are not necessarily that of the publisher.

All photography was used with the permission of the photographers and cannot be used, or reproduced without the express written permission of the photographer.

*This work is dedicated to my husband Daryl, who always encouraged
me to follow my dreams.*

Chapter 1

"What'cha doin' mister?"

Dillon Hanley looked up from where he was painting and glanced behind him. Peeking over the white picket fence was a little girl with the biggest brown eyes he had ever seen and hair the color of burnished copper. Crazy crinkly waves of it sprouted out around a freckled face.

"I'm painting this house." He explained the obvious with a wave of his paintbrush toward the object in question.

"Oh."

She didn't say anything more, so Dillon turned back to his painting, forgetting about her.

"Did Grandma Ruth say it was okay?"

"What?" Grandma Ruth? Did she mean his mother? He decided she did. "Yes, she said it was okay. She hurt her hand and couldn't finish it, so I'm doing it." Why was this kid calling his mother 'grandma?'

"How come you're painting it white?"

"Because that's the color of the rest of the house." Dillon closed his eyes, but answered patiently. He wasn't used to talking to children, would even go so far to admit he didn't have much affection for little kids. They were loud and rude and generally nuisances. He came into contact with them on a limited basis and couldn't say he spent much time with his own nephew, Ben, who was two. When he was around Ben, it was overall chaos and the whole world revolved around the little boy. It was not something he enjoyed.

"I like pink."

"What?" Dillon was jarred back to the present. "Me too. Pink is a nice color."

"Is it your fav'rite?"

"Yeah." He agreed just to stop a discussion about his favorite color.

"When are you going to be done?"

Good grief. What was this, the Inquisition?

"In a little while," Dillon answered. For a moment it was blissfully quiet with only the nearby trees rustling in the early spring Minnesota breeze. He had taken over the chore for his mother after she fell off a ladder trying to paint her front porch. Surprisingly, she had gotten most of it done before her accident, leaving Dillon to finish this side. He never wanted her to paint the bungalow she had recently purchased. He preferred that if she was going to paint it, they should hire a professional. Ruth Hanley refused. It was a project she wanted to do and that was that.

"I think I hear your mother calling," Dillon said.

She shook her head. "She's taking a bubble bath and told me to go outside and play for a little bit."

Dillon registered that and cleared his throat, dipping the paintbrush in the paint.

"Mister?"

Dillon sighed. "Yes?"

"Penny, stop bothering the man."

Dillon automatically turned to identify the source of the slightly husky, but totally feminine voice that had interrupted the little girl.

He wasn't disappointed. Standing next to Penny was a woman with the same red hair, only hers was pulled back in a high messy bun with tendrils falling around her neck. He would bet that hair was magnificent when it was down.

The rest of her already looked magnificent, Dillon decided as he took in the clear brown eyes that matched the little girl's, the finely arched eyebrows, the full pink mouth and the trim figure she presented despite the bulky sweat-shirt she was wearing and the fact that the bottom half of her was blocked by the fence. He badly wanted to see the rest of her, but didn't trust himself to move over to the fence to get a better look.

He imagined all that hair piled up as she sat in a bath full of bubbles. His body tightened in reaction.

"I'm not bothering him, really Mom. Tell her I'm not, mister," the little girl implored, bringing Dillon back to the conversation. She was the little girl's mother. That made sense. The hair gave it away. The fact that they were standing in the same yard also gave it away. He blinked his eyes in disappointment at the thought that she belonged to another man, then felt an uncomfortable stab of jealousy that the other man had seen her first. And what was that all about? he asked himself, shaking his head to clear it.

"The name is Dillon Hanley." Dillon introduced himself as he stepped over to the fence to offer his hand. When she didn't shake it, the little girl began to giggle. He looked down to see the paintbrush still clutched in his right hand.

"Sorry," he muttered, shifting the brush to the other hand and wiping his right hand on the back of his worn blue jeans before offering it again.

"I'm Jill Baxter, and this is my daughter Penny."

Jill noticed Dillon's look of disappointment after he had so blatantly taken inventory of her features. He obviously didn't find her attractive and why would she care anyway? It made her voice cooler than normal.

"Are you Grandma Ruth's little Dillon?" Penny asked in awe, her eyes even bigger than before. "You sure look big to me."

"He is big," Jill explained, "but when Ruth calls him

'little' that's just a nickname, like you're my little pumpkin." She gently tweaked a bit of Penny's hair. She wasn't lying, Jill thought, he was tall, maybe six-foot-two or so and had the muscles of a male model. His hair was the color of ripe wheat with dark streaks running through it. Cut short on the sides, waves of longer hair on top of his head defined a widow's peak Jill found adorable. His face was scruffy with a day-old beard and those brown eyes seemed to look right through her. A brush stroke of pink accented his high cheekbones.

Dillon couldn't remember the last time he blushed, but he would remember this time as Jill's eyes flicked over him. She might be married and belong to someone else but the look she gave him made him sweat as well.

"It was nice meeting you Dillon" she finally said. "Penny, I'm going to talk to Ruth for a minute. Remember, don't bother him."

"I won't Mom," came the response.

Dillon watched as Jill retreated into her yard. She walked to the front sidewalk and came around to his mother's front door, knocking before entering.

The little girl apparently took her mother seriously and was silent, so Dillon turned back to the unfinished painting project and dipped his brush into the white paint, drawing it out carefully and removing the excess before applying it to the home his mother had purchased two months earlier. He had tried to convince her to buy a condo when she decided to move from the sprawling family home his brother and wife now occupied but she wanted to have a yard and a place to plant her flowers.

Once she had seen this house in an older neighborhood in their hometown of Mankato, Minnesota, there was no changing her mind. Dillon admitted it was a good investment despite needing a few repairs, like this paint job. It was small, almost a cottage in Dillon's estimation, but it was perfect for his mother. It was a on a shady street and the other homes in the neighborhood were well-kept. He had noticed toys in several of the yards, which indicated a young neighborhood, something that appealed to his mother when she was making her choice.

Now that she was getting older, she wanted to be surrounded by younger people, to help keep her young, she claimed. No retirement home for her, Ruth Hanley said, she was only in her late sixties and perfectly able to take care of herself.

He supposed she had met the child who had just bombarded him with questions. She liked to make friends and loved children. She tried to spend as much time with her grandson Ben as she could.

Dillon shuddered. Children. The thought of having to live next door to them was enough to make him happy he had chosen his home, a modern townhouse, in a neighborhood where few children ventured. It was affluent, near the golf course and quiet. If there were children around, Dillon wasn't aware of them.

He should have insisted his mother hire someone to do the painting, Dillon thought idly, then his mother wouldn't have fallen off the ladder and fractured her wrist. In his defense, he didn't know she intended to paint it herself, until after the fact. And now here he was, spending this beautiful Saturday morning painting a house and talking to a little girl with bright copper hair instead of golfing with Suzanne.

Now Suzanne, he thought, she was worth a Saturday morning. A tall, willowy blond, Suzanne was as comfortable on a golf course as she was in a glass-walled executive office. She was a proud, quiet woman with brown eyes that held secrets. He saw her in a business suit during the week as she ran her own accounting business, but she was also stunning in golf attire or an evening gown. In fact, she was worth a whole Saturday and Sunday too.

"Hey mister, did Grandma Ruth say it was okay to get paint on you?"

Dillon glanced down at his paint-spattered jeans and noticed for the first time he was being a little sloppy. He looked back at the board that now sported about three coats of paint. He groaned at himself for his lack of concentration. Of course, Suzanne could do that to him. Probably Jill Baxter could too, but he wouldn't let himself think of her. She was married. Suzanne wasn't.

"Yes, Grandma Ruth said it was okay," he answered the little girl who showed no signs of leaving, "and you can call me Dillon if you want."

Her brown eyes got bigger. "Really? Cool."

There was silence for a moment.

"Can I help you paint?" she asked. "I'm very good at it. I'm in first grade and I can paint all sorts of pictures."

Dillon considered. "I'm almost done here so there's not much more to do," he said, "and I'm not sure your mom would be okay with that."

Penny sighed in disappointment. "That's what Grandma Ruth said last week," she said. "She told me to stay right where I was, 'cause Mom would be mad if I got paint on me."

Dillon grinned. His mother never let him get paint-spattered when he was that age either. He looked at his jeans. She might even have something to say about it now. He considered the little face on the other side of the fence.

"Didn't your mother tell you not to talk to strangers?"

Penny just giggled and Dillon knew he had lost. He could count on her company for the duration. There was quiet for a few minutes.

"I don't have a dad either."

"What?" Dillon admitted he didn't have much experience with children, but he knew there had to be some sense behind that statement. "You don't have a dad?"

"Well, I have a dad but he doesn't live here. I never met him. He went to California," Penny explained with a sigh. "He didn't want me, so he left. He got married to someone else. And Grandma Ruth said your dad went to Heaven. So we don't have dads together."

It took Dillon a minute to absorb that news. She had a dad, of course she did, but he didn't live here. She never met him. Dillon considered the turn of events. Interesting. Jill Baxter was divorced? Her ex-husband lived in California? He wondered why his mother never mentioned her neighbor. She was big on matchmaking and introduced him to single women all the time. It was maddening, Dillon thought. He didn't need a matchmaker. His life was close to perfect.

Jill Baxter just became much more interesting.

Whoa, Dillon told himself. She might be interesting but so was Suzanne. His mother's next-door neighbor also came with another person. A very short person who talked all the time and asked questions one after the other. So, maybe not. He would stick with Suzanne.

"I guess that's right, we don't."

Penny apparently didn't have any more observations to make so Dillon painted in silence for a few minutes while Penny hung on the fence and watched. He was finally concentrating on the job at hand and didn't notice the car that stopped at the curb or see the little girl who bounced over and perched next to Penny.

"What'cha doin' mister?"

Dillon turned, startled by the question. "Penny, I thought we..."

He closed his eyes and shook his head, then rubbed his free hand across his forehead. Sunstroke, already? Dillon opened his eyes. No, there were still two of them. He put his brush down and bent to take a closer look at the identical faces peering at him over the fence. Amazing!

"He's painting Grandma Ruth's house, can't you see?" the one on the right answered. She must be Penny.

"This is my friend Peggy," Penny pronounced. "Peggy, this is Dillon. He said I could call him that." She nodded.

Yes, the one on the right was definitely Penny, but he was sure they were identical. Both were even dressed the same, in tennis shoes, jeans and purple and white striped sweat shirts. God help him if they moved.

"Twins?"

Dillon didn't realize he'd spoken aloud until the girl on the left... Peggy... answered. Both girls giggled.

"No mister." She looked at him like that would explain everything and pointed to a tall, red-haired woman going up the walk to Penny's home.

She was wearing a white skirt and yellow blazer with a patterned yellow silky blouse beneath it, and looked very, very regal, right down to her yellow high heels. Her hair, the same burnished copper of the little girls', fell in waves to her shoulders. Brown eyes met his as she approached. Jill? How had she done that? He was sure she hadn't come out of his mother's house. But if it wasn't Jill, it had to be her twin sister. She looked exactly like Jill, from the hair to the brown eyes and laughing smile. They were in their late twenties maybe?

Dillon straightened, acknowledging her with a nod. He didn't trust himself to speak. Now he knew what Jill looked like dressed up. The girls were clearly from the same mold and if that was any indication, they would break more than a few hearts when they got older.

"Girls, don't be bothering the man, he's trying to paint," she admonished in the same husky voice Jill had used. "Penny, where's your mother?"

"She's talking to Grandma Ruth," the girl on the left answered. Had they moved? Dillon hadn't noticed. He was quickly going insane.

"Hi, I'm Dillon Hanley, Ruth's son." Dillon remembered his manners and offered a paint-spattered hand across the fence, then thought better of it as he took another look at her clothes. "Sorry."

"Ah," was her only comment. He wanted to ask about that one word, but she was continuing. Maybe he was better off this way, Dillon decided, not knowing what she meant.

"I'm Jan Humphrey, Jill Baxter's sister and Peggy's mother." She patted the head of the girl on the left. "Well, I've got to run, I need to talk to Jill for a minute before I leave. It was nice to meet you, Dillon. Remember girls, no bothering him."

"We won't," they replied in unison to Jan's back as she headed toward Ruth Hanley's front door. They giggled together.

"You goin' to paint some more?" one of the youngsters asked. He wasn't sure which and decided not to ask.

In fact, Dillon wasn't sure who he was or what he was doing anymore. He finally pulled himself together, closed his mouth, and attempted to answer the question. What was it?

"Ah, yes, I'm going to paint some more." I think, he added to himself as he looked at them to be sure they were still both there and identical. They were.

Only a moment later, Ruth Hanley poked her head around the corner of the house.

She was a small woman with hair that was nearly white, cut and styled to frame her face, just touching her shoulders. The glasses covering intelligent eyes were modern and complemented her face. She was the perfect mother, slim and graceful, and full of laughter. His father had been tall and wiry. He had often said his sons got their intelligence from her, thank God. There was no doubt about it, Ruth Hanley was smart, except on days when she decided to do things like paint her own house. Or doing it standing on an unstable ladder.

"Hi girls, would you like some lemonade?" Ruth Hanley asked.

"Yes," the girls answered in unison. Again. They started to climb over the fence.

"Good. Dillon?"

"What? Oh no, not now. I'll come in just a few minutes." He didn't need lemonade, he needed a stiff shot of whiskey. Dillon put the now-drying paintbrush down, wiped his hands on his jeans and helped the girls over the fence. He was never going to get this chore done.

Before he let them go, Dillon had to ask, "I thought your mothers said to stay in the yard?"

"That doesn't include Grandma Ruth's, but we have to be invited, Mom says," answered the one Dillon assumed to be Penny.

"See ya," the other one shouted as they rounded the corner of the house.

Dillon turned his attention back to the house and was finally concentrating on the job at hand when he heard someone shout his name. It was his mother, telling him to take a break. Dillon decided right then that the rest of the paint job was going to be finished in the next five minutes or he would call the professionals first Monday morning.

The little girls were sitting on the kitchen floor eating cookies and drinking their lemonade when Dillon entered. His mother and the young women were sitting at the kitchen table chatting as Dillon went to the sink to wash up. He had made a pass at the paintbrush and his hands with the hose, but had decided they needed soap as well as water.

His mother introduced Dillon to her guests as he dried his hands.

"Jan, Jill, this is my son, Dillon. He's the president of First Mankato Bank. He took over when my husband died. Anyway, Dillon, this is Jill Baxter who lives next door and her sister, Jan Humphrey."

Dillon nodded to Jan and Jill. "We talked outside," he said. "It's nice to meet you again."

Then he made the connection. Cousins. The little girls were cousins, but Dillon couldn't help asking the next question.

"Twins?" He looked closer at the two women. At least these two wore different clothes, for they were as identical as the two youngsters.

"As a matter of fact, no," Jan answered as she held out her hand to Dillon. He shook it lightly, then did the same to Jill. He didn't really pay attention to Jan's reply because when his fingers touched Jill Baxter's hand, a jolt of awareness shot through his body. Apparently, she felt it too. They looked in surprise at one another before Dillon hastily dropped her hand. He quickly turned away so no one would notice and leaned up against the counter, stretching his long legs out in front of him.

Jill sat very still. How, in the space of a few seconds and one touch, could this near stranger turn her insides to quivering jelly? She had seen pictures of him in Ruth Hanley's living room, but they did little justice to the real-life man. A clean-cut jaw, broad shoulders and narrow hips. *How do his jeans stay up?* she wondered. Arms golden brown and looking like he spent hours in the gym. A bank president? He didn't look like any bank president she knew. *What would his chest look like? Stop that, Jill Baxter!* She focused her attention on his words.

"Mom, the painting is done. Is there anything else around here that needs done while I'm here?" He helped himself to a cookie and took the glass of lemonade his mother offered. He still thought whiskey might be the better drink.

Ruth Hanley and Jan had exchanged speculative glances during the handshake, noting Dillon's inattention to Jan's answer and the speed with which Jill and Dillon dropped one another's hand.

He was sure at some point his mother had referred to her neighbor as a bit eccentric and a little on the dumpy side. Jill Baxter was neither. Dillon sipped his lemonade and tuned out the conversation they were having. And what, divorced? Why would any man in his right man let a woman like Jill Baxter get away? Just looking at her made Dillon's stomach tighten again. He didn't show that in his stance, however, he forced himself to relax.

"What do you think?"

"That sounds fine," Dillon absently answered his

mother before he realized he had no idea what she was talking about. He hoped he didn't just agree to put another coat of paint on the house, because he wasn't doing that, but there was no way he was going to admit that he hadn't been listening.

His hopes were dashed in the next instant as he noticed knowing smiles on the women's faces, and the girls giggled behind their hands and jumped up, nearly spilling their drinks. They embraced and bounced up and down.

"Well, that's great. Can you girls be ready by six-thirty?"

Ruth Hanley addressed Peggy and Penny, who stopped giggling long enough to answer solemnly, "Yes, Grandma Ruth, we'll be ready." They giggled again, then grabbed their plastic glasses and put them on the counter next to Dillon.

"Thank you," one of them told Dillon. He wasn't going to guess who it was. She hugged his legs. "We love the circus."

Circus? What circus? What was she talking about? He just agreed to take two six-year-olds to the circus? On a Saturday night? He must have, because they had stopped bouncing and were looking at him with expectation in those big brown eyes.

"Um..." He looked at his mother for help. She smiled broadly but didn't say anything. Now what? He decided to give in gracefully. Maybe Suzanne liked the circus too. "I do too." That's what he got for letting his mind wander to the woman with the glorious red hair looking expectantly at him.

"Do you like cotton candy?" he asked the girls. What the heck, Dillon decided, he hadn't been to a circus in years.

Maybe it would be fun.

They squealed in excitement, jumping up and down and shouting at each other about everything they were going to see at the circus when Jill finally decided to have pity on the man. He was clearly uncomfortable about the circus idea, even though he was trying to be a good sport about it.

Of course, if Dillon had been listening to his mother instead of leering at her, he wouldn't be in this mess now, Jill thought. All Ruth had wanted to know was if he thought the eaves needed cleaning. When it was obvious he wasn't listening, Ruth had given the young girls a conspiring look, and asked if they would be ready at six-thirty. Penny had added the circus on her own, knowing Grandma Ruth was playing a joke on her son. By agreeing, Dillon took the joke away and made it real for the children.

Jill sighed, knowing she would be making a trip to the circus on a Saturday night. What difference did it make that she didn't have any plans? She had never had a real fondness for the circus. Maybe she should let him sweat it out a while longer. She smiled questioningly at her sister who nodded.

"Girls," Jan said gently, "why don't you go wash your hands and faces and then go back outside and play?" They were out of the kitchen before Jan finished her question, obviously ignoring the first part of the request. Jill decided clean hands weren't that important if they were going to play in the dirt.

"But stay in Ruth's yard," Jill added for good measure. "And don't touch that wet paint."

They heard a faint 'we won't' as the front door slammed shut. Dillon shook his head as the women grinned at one another, knowing those words were the girls' stock answer to everything.

"Where do they get all that energy?" he wondered aloud.

"That's a good question," Ruth answered. "I do remember a certain little boy and his brother who spent many days playing and running until I thought I would drop from exhaustion just watching them." She looked pointedly at her son. "Now, about the circus..."

At that point, Jill and Jan rose almost as one from the table and placed their empty glasses on the counter, deciding it was time to leave. They both knew Ruth and had an idea was what was coming. Dillon hadn't moved and Jill brushed his arm as she placed her glass next to her sister's. He inhaled the clean, cool scent of her and again pictured her in a bubble bath. It was enough to make him stop listening to the conversation and concentrate on making his body's responses behave.

"Thanks for the lemonade Ruth," Jan said as she gave the older woman a kiss on the cheek. "I would love to stay and chat, but the real estate business calls." She checked the time on her watch.

"I think I should check on the girls," Jill added. "It was nice meeting you Dillon." Nice? The man was a walking fantasy. Wide shoulders, narrow hips, long legs. Stop it, Baxter. He's not in your league. Ruth had mentioned her unmarried son on several occasions in the two months they had known each other, usually in connection with the country club he belonged to or the important people he was dining with that particular night.

"And don't worry about the circus," she added to be charitable. "I can take the girls if they really want to go." She could just see him and his date with two little girls at the circus, because she was sure he wasn't spending his Saturday night home alone or taking two six-year-olds to a circus alone. His high-society date would probably never speak to him again, regardless of the fact that he was president of a bank.

Jill didn't give Dillon a chance to answer as she told Ruth goodbye. She gave the older woman a kiss as well, then left with her sister.

Ruth sighed as the girls disappeared from view. She turned to Dillon as the front door closed softly. "If I had ever been blessed with daughters, I would have wanted them just like those two," she said, almost to herself.

"But Mom, you have a daughter-in-law, and you've always said she was the daughter you never had." Dillon was surprised to hear the wistfulness in her voice. She had never uttered an ill word about his brother Jason's wife, Meredith. In fact, Meredith often said that if all mothers-in-law were as wonderful as Ruth Hanley, there would never be any mother-in-law jokes.

Ruth looked at her son as though she had forgotten his presence. She laughed guiltily. "Of course she is, but can't I be greedy and ask for a daughter or two?" She considered her son seriously. "As a matter of fact, Jill isn't married. Her husband left her just after Penny was born..."

"Don't even think it, Mom," Dillon warned as something inside him involuntarily jumped with joy at the news that Jill Baxter was definitely divorced. "No match making."

Ruth Hanley looked wounded. "I wouldn't presume to matchmake for you, if that's what you mean," she said. "I was just making conversation. I know you prefer those women who hang on every word you say and think 'baby' is a four-letter word."

"It is a four-letter word." Dillon smiled.

"You know what I mean."

"I do, and that's the trouble. Now, what am I going to do about two six-year-olds and a circus?" Despite Jill Baxter's statement that he didn't have to go to the circus, Dillon knew he wouldn't get out of that easily where his mother was concerned. He also didn't go back on his word once he gave it.

In the next yard, Jill sat back on her heels and surveyed her handiwork. It wouldn't be long now and she would have a beautiful flower garden along the part of her front porch where the low bushes at the corner of the house stopped. The last of the weeds were gone and the flowers she and Penny had planted the previous week were starting to poke through the ground. Penny was supposed to help her with the weeding, but Jill decided the flowers were safer with the young girls playing on the playset in the backyard. They could hardly wait to go to the circus that evening, even though she had explained that she would be taking them instead of Dillon Hanley. The circus was the circus and they didn't care who took them.

She wiped her brow with her sleeve and smiled as she recalled the look of surprise on the man's face when he discovered his plans for the evening. He was probably breathing deep sighs of relief that she had let him off the hook. She wished she could see him breathing deeply, Jill thought. That t-shirt he was wearing gave evidence of muscles that were well developed. She wondered how he kept in such good shape. She recalled that Ruth mentioned he was a banker, so he didn't get his body by swinging a hammer or moving heavy merchandise. Maybe he snuck into the vault and hefted money sacks on his noon hour.

Jill smiled to herself at the picture that presented as she

bent to finish cultivating the earth surrounding the tender plants. She should go in and get lunch ready for the girls. She swore they had bottomless pits for stomachs and it wouldn't be long before they were asking for something to eat. Of course, the cookies and lemonade at Ruth's and then the fruit she had given them a few minutes ago might hold them for a little while.

Jan and Jill traded babysitting on Saturdays so the girls had a chance to play together. Jill seldom worked on weekends during the summer, but often on Saturdays Jan showed homes to couples who couldn't get away during the week.

In fact, it was Jan who sold Ruth the house next door to Jill. Jill had been relieved when an older woman had expressed interest in the small home. She didn't want some weirdo living next door. Now, after only a couple of months, it felt like she had known Ruth all of her life. Ruth didn't mind having Penny and occasionally Peggy underfoot. Instead she encouraged the youngsters to visit and had recently talked about keeping them while their mothers worked.

Jill pondered the idea as she broke up the soil, and was considering how it would work when she noticed the old, tattered pair of tennis shoes standing at the edge of her flower bed. She looked up and her gaze caught a pair of paint-spattered, tight-fitting blue jeans. And that t-shirt, still hinting at what lay beneath.

He looked impatient, tapping one foot by the time she got to his face, noting the firm jaw, the straight nose and thick eyebrows, drawn together now as he frowned. Maybe he didn't like to be leered at, she thought. Whatever it was, Dillon Hanley was not a happy man, Jill decided as she sat back on her heels to gaze up at his set expression.

"I'll take you to the circus, but I won't marry you," he ground out.

Chapter 2

"Excuse me?" Jill asked, confused.

"I said, I'm not marrying you," Dillon repeated.

"Well, that's what I thought you said," Jill replied, rising to her feet. "I'm not sure why, and I didn't even ask to you to take me to the circus, but that sounds fine to me." Jill smiled serenely at him. What on earth had Ruth Hanley said to her son?

"What?"

"It really isn't necessary to marry me, but if you want to take the girls and I to the circus, that's fine. I figured I would want to come along. I just met you and despite being Ruth's son, my daughter and niece aren't going anywhere with you alone. As for getting married, I have no intentions to marry anyone, especially you."

Dillon squinted his brown eyes at her. She had no intentions of marrying him? What?

"And I would prefer next time you wait until I propose before you turn me down," she calmly continued.

He opened his mouth to speak, then decided to shut it. For someone who had always prided himself on being in control in any given situation, he was doing poorly. Every time he opened his mouth today he got in trouble. He focused his attention on the woman standing in front of him. She knelt down and returned to her task. She was methodically turning over the dirt in the flower bed. He glimpsed the smallest of smiles curving her lips.

"It isn't funny, you know."

"Isn't it?" Jill asked. "According to you, your mother already has us engaged and about to walk down the aisle whether we want it or not. Next thing you know, she'll have us producing grandchildren just for her."

Jill couldn't resist a full smile. She doubted Ruth could force her son to do anything he didn't want, especially something like producing offspring. Had Ruth even said anything of the sort? Jill doubted it. She wasn't sure why he was worked up, but he clearly was.

"It really is funny," Jill replied. She looked up at him. "I'm sorry," she said, laughing and clearly not sorry, "but you have to realize that I don't get marriage proposals, or rather non-marriage proposals, or whatever that was, turned down every day."

She had a beautiful smile, absolutely gorgeous, Dillon decided. She smiled with not only her mouth, but her whole face. He could even detect a mischievous twinkle in her eyes, something he didn't see every day. No, stop, he told himself and in the next second smiled back at her, unable to resist.

"Just as long as you realize what she's up to," he said.

"I have no idea what she's up to," Jill replied. "Did Ruth actually say she wanted us to get married, because it seems a bit presumptuous and I have never thought Ruth was presumptuous. I can't see her saying anything like that."

Dillon finally forced himself to admit he may have acted prematurely. Possibly immaturely as well. After all, he was the one who fell into the circus trap. And now he was taking two little girls to the circus. Sure, she said she was coming along which he supposed was better, but he didn't think spending time with any of them was a good idea. And he already had plans for the evening.

"And I do know what she's up to," Jill replied. "While I don't think she's matchmaking, it's been 'Dillon this and my boy that' for weeks. So far I've managed to take it lightly.

I suggest you do too. After all, she can't matchmake if neither of us is interested."

"You're not?" Dillon couldn't help but feel disappointed. Why wouldn't she be? He was used to women being interested in him. It happened all the time. And Jill Baxter was definitely, even dressed as she was, a woman, he thought. His gaze took in her silky hair, pulled away from a perfect face. Her brown eyes, framed by long, dark lashes, were filled with laughter. His gaze moved from there down to her breasts, covered demurely by her sweatshirt, to her hips, snuggled by those jeans.

She shrugged her shoulders, trying not to show her discomfort at his perusal. Instead, she gathered her gardening gloves and tools and rose again.

"Of course not," she assured him. *Liar. You've got that entire body memorized.* "I'm very happy with my life. I can't see any reason to disrupt it now."

"Disrupt?"

"Yes, you know, wreak havoc with, confuse, meander from the path I've chosen?"

Dillon closed his eyes in mock despair. "I know what the word means." He looked into her eyes, which surprisingly, hit about level with his own. He hadn't realized she was that tall. She turned and walked to the porch and sat down on the top step. He followed.

"I just haven't heard myself ever described as disruptive. Other than by my mother or my third grade teacher," he amended, grinning broadly. "I'm very stable, predictable even."

"Never mind. I was just trying to assure you that if you walk away right now, your mother will understand that matchmaking won't work with us," Jill said. "I doubt she's serious about the matchmaking, or whatever you think she's doing, considering how long she's lived here. I'll take the girls to the circus."

"Why do you think she's not matchmaking?" Dillon asked as he sat beside her, ignoring her suggestion that he leave. He was interested despite his earlier remarks. Or maybe in spite of, he wasn't sure.

"Well, consider this. If she were truly matchmaking, she would have invited us both over for dinner one evening and then contrived a way for us to be alone. She hasn't done that, has she?"

Dillon considered. No, she hadn't. Why hadn't she, though? Did his mother think it was fair to keep this gorgeous, and if this conversation was anything to go by, intriguing, woman to herself? Why hadn't she even mentioned Jill Baxter to him? She apparently talked about him to her. He was losing it. He was interested and he didn't want to be. He wanted her to be interested too. He just didn't want anyone, even his mother, interfering in his life. It was fine the way it was.

He glanced at her, another question on his lips. Jill was leaning back, lifting her face to the sun, her eyes closed, the rise and fall of her breasts evident against the tautness of her sweatshirt where it was pulled tight by the way she was sitting. And her throat. Exposed to the sun and his view, soft and white, begging to be explored.
She didn't move when he cleared his throat.

"Jill?"

"Hmm?"

"Are you asleep?"

She opened her eyes and straightened up. Dillon was instantly sorry he said anything.

"No, I was just taking advantage of the quiet."

"Quiet?" Dillon looked around. Yes, he guessed it was quiet, for a city. There were still birds chirping, cars driving by and the sound of children playing, but it was peaceful.

"Yes, it won't be long before the girls are back, wanting lunch," Jill explained.

"Oh, that kind of quiet." He grinned at her. "The bubble bath kind of quiet."

She swung around to look at him in surprise. "How did you know about my bubble bath?"

"Would you believe I peeked through the window?" he asked with a wicked grin.

"Penny, huh?" She smiled back at him as he nodded.

"How do you tell those two apart?" Dillon asked, clearing his throat. His body desperately needed the subject changed to something less suggestive than bubble baths.

"Do you know how many times I've been asked that?" Jill leaned back again, making Dillon's heart beat faster as her form was once again revealed. He forced himself to concentrate on the conversation.

"Thousands probably," he tried to answer affably, "but I'd still like to know."

She opened one eye to look at him. "For one, I'm Penny's mother. For another, I've lived with her for six years. And," she added, "if you get to know them, Peggy and Penny have different personalities." Jill shrugged. "You just have to watch them a while."

"And lucky me, I get the chance."

Jill heard sarcasm in his voice and frowned. "You are lucky. They don't often get to go somewhere special with a grownup other than Jan and Grant or myself. The circus is an unexpected treat for them, and I promise they'll be on their best behavior. I've already said you didn't need to take them." She didn't need to cross her fingers, she expected to be there to ensure that they were good.

Dillon looked at the anger on her face with concern. "Hey, I was kidding. They seem like wonderful kids. I will definitely take them to the circus. I said I would and I will." Of course, what he knew about kids was limited to his own childhood and what little he saw of his brother's little boy. Terrors! He cleared his throat and changed the subject again.

"I take it Penny doesn't get to see her father often."

Jill stiffened, and Dillon knew he had made a tactical error.

"Why would you think that?"

"She said he went to California..."

"My, you two had quite the conversation, didn't you?"

Dillon turned to look at her seriously. "I'm just trying to figure out why in the world any man in his right mind would leave a beautiful woman like you."

Jill smiled, acknowledging the compliment. "Maybe he wasn't."

"Wasn't what?" Why did he feel he was losing his grip on reality today?

"In his right mind. That's what I decided a long time ago."

"You mean your husband really was crazy?" Dillon was incredulous.

"Not really, but when he left the day Penny was born, I was devastated," Jill confided. "I needed a reason to give myself for his actions. After all, it was his first affair, but when he said he was leaving me, I just couldn't let myself think I wasn't enough of a woman for him. And I had literally just had a baby. His baby."

"The jerk. He left you for another woman right after you had his baby?" Dillon asked. The man was crazy, he thought.

"Worse."

"Worse than leaving you for another woman on the day you had his baby?" Dillon looked incredulous. "What could possibly be worse? You don't mean he left you for another man?" he asked, attempting to lighten the mood.

Jill nodded seriously, leaving Dillon stunned and speechless. "I knew our marriage wasn't like normal couples', certainly not like Jan's," she explained. "Ron didn't have much interest in sex, but we were good friends. It was working. And then it wasn't."

Why she was going into this with someone she had known for such a short time? Jill wasn't sure, but suddenly it was important to share the details with someone other than her family. With Dillon Hanley.

"Our marriage was comfortable, but before Penny was born, he met someone. A man." She talked, unconscious of the pain in her voice. "He told me they fell in love." Jill turned to Dillon. "I thought Ron and I loved each other, but he decided that marriage wasn't right for him. That women weren't right for him. And he left. He's never been back."

"Wow." What else could he say?

Jill smiled at him. "Pretty weird, I know, but that's what happened. He packed up and they moved to California, unable to accept the criticism of his family here in Minnesota," she said. "His family was not happy. And I'm lucky," she added seriously. "At least he never slept with a guy until then."

Dillon was silent for a moment, unsure what to say. I'm sorry? He was sorry that something like this had happened to her, but he wasn't sorry Jill wasn't married. Dillon thought he would like to get to know Jill Baxter better. Stop, stop, stop, he told himself. She may not have a husband, but she had a child and he didn't think children were any more of an option for him than for her first husband.

"How was he able to leave his newborn daughter?" Dillon asked. "That's seems harsh."

Jill shrugged. "He only saw her once, when she was born," she said. "He wouldn't even hold her."

Dillon could do nothing but shake his head.

"And his parents, they live here in Mankato?" He didn't recall hearing of any Baxters, but then again, Jill lived here and he hadn't known her.

"No, Minneapolis. We lived there too. I only moved here to be closer to Jan." She smiled wryly. "I guess I ran away too, but I like it here." Jill looked around her at the neat homes and the clean neighborhood. Dillon followed her gaze. "I would never have made it without Jan and her moral support."

"It's a good place to raise a child," he conceded. As long as it's someone else and not Dillon Hanley doing the raising of said child, he thought

"That's why we're still here." Jill shrugged her shoulders. "It's also a good place to run a business."

"You own a business?"

She nodded and started to speak, only to have Dillon forestall her.

"Then surely we should have met? Haven't you ever

needed a loan?"

"I'm in one of those businesses where you don't need a loan to get started." Jill laughed.

"This doesn't sound good," Dillon mumbled.

"No wait, I didn't mean it like that," Jill said, laughing again. I'm a house sitter."

"A house sitter?"

"Yes, you know, I look after people's houses when they go to south in the winter. Make sure the pipes don't freeze and all that?"

Dillon breathed an exaggerated sigh of relief. "You had me worried there for a minute. How did you get started in...house sitting, you called it?"

"I guess it's really property management," Jill explained. "Anyway, Penny and I came to stay with Jan for a few days. I needed a new start and I needed an income. Her neighbors were leaving for Arizona and hated to leave their house empty, so Penny and I stayed there through the winter. They were so happy with the condition of their house when they got back that they kept me on and recommended me to their friends. Now I have a pretty good business. I also manage a few properties that are rented out for a few days at a time."

"As in AirBnB?" he asked. "Can you actually make money doing that?" The banker in him wanted to know. "Doesn't that leave you with a lot of free time?"

"As a matter of fact, no. The Kanowskys, Jan's neighbors, decided they liked to travel, knowing their property was being taken care of, so I have them, and several others, year round."

"But enough about me," she said, looking at her watch. "This has been fun but don't you think it's time you went home, before your mother thinks we're engaged?"

Dillon looked stricken as he glanced toward his mother's house. He saw a curtain move slightly and realized he was having a nice time just having a conversation with Jill Baxter. "Damn. You're right." He rose from the step, then turned and offered her his hand.

She shook her head. "I think I'll stay here until the troops come looking for me," she said. "I'm surprised they haven't already come looking for lunch."

"All right then, I'll see you all at six-thirty." He accepted the fact that she was coming along, he expected nothing less, knowing and understanding her background. He actually thought having her along might be better. He certainly didn't mind her company.

He considered for a moment, then asked, "Am I supposed to pick Peggy up here or at her house?"

"Peggy is staying here today, but Dillon," she felt compelled to explain, "the girls were pulling your leg to get you back for not paying attention to your mother." Jill decided it was past time to tell him the whole story. "It isn't necessary for you to take them to the circus tonight. And don't tell me you don't have anything better to do on a Saturday night."

"Mom already explained about the circus, but I was serious when I said I would take them and as long as it's all right with you, I will." He cocked his head to one side. "I haven't been to a circus in years," he added wistfully, "It might be fun."

Fun? Jill laughed. He had no idea how much fun a Saturday night spent with two young girls could be.

Dillon decided to ignore her knowing laugh. "I do appreciate you saying you will come." As much as he hated to admit it, and he never would, Dillon was interested in the warm and gentle woman who could sit contentedly on a porch step, not worrying about impressing a man.

Jill considered, relishing the sound of his voice. An evening with one of the best-looking men she had met for a long time. And Dillon Hanley was handsome. Not in the overly perfected way her husband Ron had been, but rugged. He looked good in old clothes and would probably look just as good in a tuxedo. Ron would never have worn old clothes, spattered with paint. He had been too afraid of the image he presented. He always wanted to impress the people they knew.

Dillon interrupted her thoughts. He wasn't sure he liked the way she was looking at him. Leering. Again. Never mind that he had done the same thing to her. He just wasn't used to being leered at. He pulled his keys out of his pocket and looked over at his mother's house. "Look, I've got to get going. I'll be back."

He was gone before Jill had a chance to answer. She waved and watched him drive away in a shiny white pickup truck.

By the time Jill answered Dillon's ring at the door that evening, she was ready to stay home. She had made the girls take naps and baths and eat some dinner, and now they were all set for the circus, jumping up and down and dashing to the door every few minutes to see if Dillon was there. In fact, Jill was surprised she made it to the door ahead of the girls, even though she had sent them to go to the bathroom one more time before they left. The circus was being held under a big top tent and if Jill's guess was correct, she wasn't going to want to try and find a bathroom once there.

Dillon looked good in blue jeans and a knit shirt,

Jill decided as she invited him inside. Very good. He was no longer paint-spattered and his hair looked like he had just come from a modeling job. It made Jill want to run her fingers through it. Still, he didn't remind her of the almost too perfect image of her ex-husband. He smelled wonderful too, of aftershave. It made Jill want to get closer as he greeted Peggy and Penny with hugs. He really had no choice about the hugs, Jill decided, chuckling, as the girls almost bowled him over. She collected their jackets and started them out the door.

"I'll have them back early, just as soon as the circus is over," Dillon told Jill.

"Oh, I was serious about coming along," Jill replied.

"Don't you trust me with them?"

"I thought we had this conversation earlier." Jill laughed, causing a current of sensation to run through Dillon's body. "Of course I trust you." She turned off the light and started out the door, indicating to Dillon that he was to follow so she could lock the door. "It's them I don't trust with you. Are we taking your truck? Unless we drive my SUV, we're going to have to move car seats," she added.

Dillon breathed a sigh of relief. He hadn't realized he was holding his breath. He was sure she would change her mind about going. And he wasn't sure why it was important that he have this woman's trust with her child, but it was.

Jill was continuing. "I know what two small children can do to a unsuspecting, sane adult in a few hours, and I decided you didn't deserve that fate." Never mind that the idea of spending an evening with him had become more and more appealing as the day progressed. A thought suddenly occurred to her. "You don't mind if I come along, do you?" she asked as she opened the back door of her SUV to start moving car seats.

Dillon couldn't resist admiring the view she presented. She wore blue jeans and a blouse instead of the sweatshirt she had worn earlier, along with a pair of black flat shoes, showing bare ankles. Her hair was flowing past her shoulders, just like Jan's had been, and was just as magnificent. She was magnificent. He cleared his throat. Behave, he told himself.

"Let me get that," Dillon offered belatedly as he took the first car seat. Jill got the second seat, then stopped. She was looking at him questioningly. What had she asked him? Oh yeah.

"Mind? No, you know I don't." He looked into her eyes and time stood still for a moment as the awareness they had felt earlier returned, stronger this time. Jill parted her lips in expectation, feeling the draw of his lips.

"Can we go now? Can we go?" Peggy and Penny jumped up and down in unison, realizing the adults were losing focus.

Nothing could kill a possible romantic moment like two six-year-olds eager to be on their way to the circus, Dillon decided. He met Jill's smile with one of his own. He was sure she was thinking the same thing. They installed the car seats in the back seat of his pickup and Jill buckled them in.

"So, how come I've never met you?" Dillon asked over the chattering from the backseat as they pulled out of the driveway.

"Probably because I don't bank at First Mankato." She named Dillon's bank.

"You don't?" He looked hurt.

"Sorry, but when I moved here I didn't know you

worked there."

"And now?"

"Maybe I should move all of my accounts," Jill suggested. "Not that they would make much difference to a bank as big as First Mankato. I only make enough to make life comfortable for Penny and myself."

"Hey, every penny counts."

"Ugh." Jill shook her head in mock dismay as Penny spoke up from the backseat.

"Did you hear that, Mom? Ev'ry Penny counts. That's funny. One, two, three, four." She turned to Dillon. "I can count to a hundred, did you know that?" She proceeded to show them her abilities. Of course, then Peggy had to demonstrate as well. Jill just smiled and shrugged her shoulders when Dillon looked at her questioningly. Any more chance of personal conversation was lost as Dillon pulled into the area designated for circus goers.

By the time he had purchased tickets and ushered his group to their seats through the throng of excited children and their parents, Dillon was worried about his reputation and his sanity. On top of that, he was already exhausted. He shook his head. What had he been thinking? It was bad enough that he had to change his plans for the night. Instead of going out with friends, including Suzanne, he was here. He hadn't actually told Suzanne why he needed to cancel. She wouldn't have believed him anyway.

"I doubt there's one single person besides me here," he told Jill as they watched the people coming through the tent flaps. Penny and Peggy were sitting in between the two adults, which was a good idea, Dillon decided. This way he wouldn't be sitting in public in torment, touching Jill, shoulder to shoulder, hip to hip... Stop it, Hanley, or you'll be needing an excuse to leave early.

Jill laughed. She could see what he meant. On this Saturday night there were only families waiting for the clowns and the elephants to make their entrance. She decided not to point out that she was single as well. Anyway, Dillon didn't seem to be expecting an answer, Jill decided as she glanced at the man seated next to Peggy. His attention was apparently back on the crowd.

Actually, Dillon could care less about the crowd. He was fighting with his body. He forced his thoughts to her laugh and decided it was one of the nicest sounds he had ever heard. He was glad she wasn't afraid to laugh, it showed self-confidence and Dillon could tell she was being sincere, not giggling at everything he said. Not that he minded hero worship, but he admitted to himself that lately the crowd at the country club was getting a little too predictable. He relaxed on the bench and decided the circus was just what he needed.

"This is great."

"Once you get used to the smell," Jill answered, wrinkling her nose. "I always forget what a circus smells like when I'm agreeing to go to one."

"You mean sawdust and canvas and popcorn?" Dillon sniffed and breathed in the mingling scents contained in the big tent. He didn't mind it at all.

"No, I mean animals that have been confined to a hot tent filled with people," Jill laughed. "Can't you smell it?"

"Smells good to me." And it did, Dillon realized. She had leaned over the girls to talk to him and was close enough to inhale the scent of her. Jill smelled the same as she had earlier, fresh and clean. He inhaled deeply, then had to tell his body to behave again.

"When are we going to see the elephants?" Peggy asked, looking at Jill.

"Yeah, Mom, where are the elephants?" Penny echoed, looking around. She quickly forgot about the elephants. "Hey Mom, there's Robby and Derick." Penny pointed out two young boys looking for a place to sit. "Robby, Derick," she shouted, standing up and waving.

"Penny, sit down."

It was too late. Ted and Mary Hendricksen and their children, Robby and Derick, had already responded to Penny's wave and waved back. Jill could see the two adults turn to one another and whisper before heading toward them.

Dillon heard her almost inaudible groan and took his gaze away from a clown making the rounds to see a family greeting Jill and the girls. The girls scrambled over Jill to sit next to the little boys, forcing her to slide over to Dillon's side. Wonderful! No. Terrible. Now they were touching. He was in agony. The Hendricksens were introducing themselves to Dillon, unasked questions on their faces.

"Dillon's mother lives next door to me and he can't resist the circus," Jill explained.

Dillon saw her crossed fingers.

"Actually, my mother lives next door to Jill and Jill can't resist the circus," he corrected happily. "I was bringing the girls and Jill insisted she be allowed to come along."

He winced at the elbow Jill jabbed into his side when two sets of eyebrows rose, but kept the smile on his face.

"What do you think you're doing?" Jill hissed in his ear.

"Enjoying the circus," Dillon replied calmly. "Has anyone ever told you you're cute when you're angry?"

"That's the oldest line in the book, Hanley..."

"Hey, look girls, here come the camels and clowns," Dillon interrupted. He leaned across Jill, laying one hand on her back, to point and she got another whiff of his after-shave.

The man is a pro, Jill Baxter, but he doesn't mean it. He's not looking for a wife, especially one with a ready-made family. She repeated that to herself as he straightened up, so that when he looked at her again, Jill had a smile ready.

"What?" Dillon saw the sudden smile and became suspicious.

"Nothing, just enjoying the circus."

He didn't believe her for a second, but let it pass. The circus was starting. He was almost as excited as the girls. He even managed to ignore the little boy behind him who kept kicking him in the back and watched the show, all the while aware of the enticing female sitting next to him. It was only minutes before vendors were moving through the crowds, shouting and trying to sell balloons and toys, cotton candy, popcorn and peanuts.

"We want some popcorn." Both girls spoke at once, as if on cue.

"Watch the ladies on the horses." She shook her head to signal that wasn't going to happen, even as Dillon flagged down a vendor. It was too late.

Jill gave Dillon a 'you'll be sorry' look, which he acknowledged with a grin.

Two hours later he was having a hard time keeping that smile in place. They were carrying the sleeping girls up the walk to Jill's house, although how they could sleep, Dillon had no idea.

"They must have enough sugar in them to start their own candy shop," he observed.

"Popcorn, peanuts, cotton candy, soft drinks. I did try to warn you," Jill said as she unlocked the door and allowed Dillon to precede her inside.

"I know, but how could I resist these sweet little things?" Dillon indicated the little girls. They really had been sweet. They were smart and funny. He really couldn't resist any of their requests.

"Resist? The cotton candy was your idea, if I remember correctly."

Dillon had the grace to look guilty as Jill led the way through the house to Penny's bedroom. They laid them on the beds, then Dillon watched as Jill wiped their faces and put on their pajamas.

"All right, I admit it. But do you know how long it's been since I had cotton candy?" He had forgotten how much he liked it.

"Long enough to have forgotten how sticky it gets," Jill answered.

"It was worth it," Dillon pronounced.

It had been too, Dillon decided as he watched Jill tuck the sleeping girls in and give them each a kiss. They both roused long enough to give Dillon a sleepy goodnight and a hug. His heart swelled as he encountered a sticky spot on Penny's cheek that Jill had missed when she washed their faces. Amazing. Only a few hours and his life had been changed. The country club would never seem the same now that he had met Penny and her family.

Her family. His family. Dillon wondered why that sounded right as he followed Jill out to the living room, giving one last glance to the two sleeping in the darkened room. Maybe he had missed something by not getting married and having children. Dillon Hanley with children? Damn. I'm one of this town's last bachelors, he told himself. I have a reputation to uphold. He shook his head in disbelief at the argument he was having with himself. A short twenty-four hours ago he would never have dreamed about taking a child to a circus, let alone having kids, a wife or a family. Hanley, you're really in trouble.

"Would you like something to drink?" Jill was asking him. "Maybe a glass of wine?"

"I would, but I'm going to run out and move car seats," Dillon replied. "I'll be back in a minute."

He was true to his word and was back by the time Jill had opened the bottle and poured two glasses.

Jill handed him one and noticed he was shaking his head.

"What's the matter?"

He ran his fingers through his hair. "You'll never believe it."

She considered briefly, then nodded. "You're probably right. I'm going to fix us a plate of cheese and crackers. Would you like some?"

"Sounds good, but let me help." He followed her to the kitchen and immediately decided following anywhere her probably wasn't a good idea. She looked good from the back. Damn, good didn't even come close. Great. Fantastically stupendous. The guy who invented jeans had Jill Baxter in mind.

When she stopped at the counter, Dillon barely avoided running into the part of her anatomy he had been admiring. Unaware of his closeness, Jill turned around to speak.

"I guess you probably don't want..."

Dillon couldn't help himself. Lips met lips with a feather touch, then tasted.

Sugar, Jill thought. He tasted like sugar. Cotton candy with a hint of wine. Good.

She didn't realize she had spoken aloud until she heard Dillon's chuckle.

"What?"

"I thought it was good too. In fact..." he dipped his lips to hers for another taste, another touch. Jill tried to keep her senses in place. It was just a kiss. No it wasn't. It was a KISS! Capital letters, exclamation point and more. And when Dillon placed his fingers in her hair to lightly caress, Jill felt the sensation right down to her toes.

"We shouldn't be doing this." She fought for reality. He didn't want to get involved, he had already said that. And neither did she. As she had pointed out earlier in the day, she was comfortable with her life. She was. And she didn't need some good-looking playboy in her life right now. She didn't want a casual affair, she wanted marriage. He didn't want marriage, he would be happy with an affair.

"Why not? We're both enjoying it."

Jill twisted away from him and he let her go. She got out cheese and a box of crackers. In truth, she didn't have an answer, but she wasn't about to admit it. She had been enjoying the kiss. That's what scared her.

"Penny and your mother are why not."

"My mother? What's she got to do with us kissing?"

"Everything." Jill set a plate from the cupboard on the counter. "If Penny catches us kissing, she will tell your mother and she will have us married and producing those children you were worried about before you can drive across town."

"Hmm, you might have a point." He put his arms across his chest and leaned against the counter, taking in the warmth and cheerfulness that the kitchen, designed much like his mother's and decorated in yellow and white, exuded. "But Penny is in bed, asleep," he reminded her.

"Be that as it may," Jill replied, "around here the walls have ears." She lowered her voice to a whisper. "Be very quiet for just a minute."

Dillon didn't hear anything but the hum of the refrigerator. It was quiet. "So?" he whispered.

Jill put her finger on her lips.

"Mom?" It was faint, but it was there. Jill smiled as Dillon raised his eyebrows.

"Mom, I hav'ta go to the bathroom." It was louder this time. They heard a thud and then footsteps running. Penny poked her head in the kitchen. "Mom, I hav'ta go to the bathroom."

"That's fine dear, go ahead. The light is on. Does Peggy have to go too?"

Penny shook her head and rubbed her eyes. "She's asleep."

"Okay, go to the bathroom and then get back in bed. I'll see you in the morning."

"Is he staying all night?" Penny cocked her head and looked at Dillon.

Dillon and Jill glanced at each other. Jill took Penny's shoulders and pointed her in the direction of the bathroom. "No he's not staying all night. Now get to the bathroom."

"All right." Penny knew when she had lost. "G'night."

"Good night," Dillon answered, but Penny was already gone. He shook his head as Jill turned back to add crackers and cheese to her plate. "She moves faster than anyone I know."

"Except Peggy," Jill added.

They laughed together and Jill took their snacks to the table.

"How did you know she would wake up?"

Jill shrugged. "Mother's instinct?"

"Right." He didn't believe her.

"Actually, she has a hard time sleeping with anyone in the house but me," Jill explained. "It doesn't happen often, and she should go to sleep now that she knows it's just you," Jill explained.

"Just me?"

"You know what I mean," Jill said. "She likes you." So do I. More than I should.

"And how about you?"

"What?"

"Do you like me?" For some reason it was important that she did. Dillon wasn't going to ask himself why right now.

"Are you pitching for a compliment?" Jill cocked her head.

"Yes."

"Oh. Well then, I guess I do."

"Do you mean it?"

"I just said I did, so I must. What about you?"

"Oh yes, I like me too."

Jill squinted her lovely brown eyes at him, then rose with her empty glass. "That's not what I meant, and you know it." She set the glass on the counter and turned to ask if he wanted another glass of wine. She almost jumped in surprise.

He was right behind her again. Was the man part Ninja, with the ability to move silently? Jill backed up to the counter. He put his hands on her waist and stepped up to her until there was only a small gap between them. He was going to kiss her again.

This time there was certainty in the kiss. Mastery. Jill realized she was being kissed by an expert, but it was so different from the chaste kisses she had shared with Ron that it almost overwhelmed her. She gasped in surprise when he nudged her lips open and took advantage to gain entrance to her mouth, exploring and tasting.

Jill quickly found she liked the intimacy, although she was inexperienced with it.

Her arms instinctively went around his neck, pulling her breasts into contact with Dillon's chest. Immediately she could feel their response as her nipples tightened and hardened. How could this happen, and so quickly? The kiss only lasted for a few seconds, or was it a few minutes, or hours? Jill didn't care as she let herself enjoy the contact with Dillon as much as her body did.

When Dillon finally raised his head to look at her, he was surprised by the expression of bemusement he found on her face.

"What's wrong? Haven't you ever been kissed like this before?" He said it jokingly, but her answer was serious.

"No." She shook her head. "I always wondered what it was like."

"You were married and you never shared a kiss like the one we just had?"

Jill shook her head again.

"He really was crazy, wasn't he?"

"Or I was. But how could I have known?" Jill asked.

"Didn't you date in high school?"

"Yes, but that doesn't mean I ever had the socks kissed off me." Jill was indignant.

"I kissed the socks off you?" Dillon looked down at her feet. "Nope, they're still on. Maybe I should try again."

"Maybe you should…"

Chapter 3

It was even better the second time, Jill decided as she responded, meeting Dillon halfway, eager to explore the taste of him, testing the sensuality that their uniting of tongues demanded. Her arms tightened around his neck even as Dillon maintain his caressing hold on her narrow waist. Until that kiss, Jill never realized how intimate a kiss could be.

As she instinctively arched in an effort to get closer, Jill could feel the effect on her senses. A mixture of after-shave and his own scent made her head spin. Her breasts tingled as her nipples tightened once more against his chest, despite the layers of clothing between them. Her legs felt like rubber, ready to collapse, but Dillon held her, his hands spanning her back, caressing through the material of her blouse. Even as Jill realized the extent of her own arousal, Dillon's arousal penetrated her senses and their mouths again became two. Dillon's ragged breathing matched her own.

"Oh my."

"I wouldn't be surprised if my socks are missing too," Dillon grinned.

They both looked down to check, but were still standing close and bumped their foreheads.

"Ouch." Jill moved back as she rubbed her forehead.

"I think I'm seeing stars now," Dillon mumbled.

"The kiss was that good?"

"No. Yes. I mean, the kiss was wonderful, beautiful..." He cut off his rambling when he noticed she was trying to suppress laughter. There was nothing to do but join her. They leaned their foreheads together, still joined together by their arms, comfortable, the sexual tension they had felt earlier gone for the moment.

Dillon sighed. "I guess I should go home."

"Probably," Jill agreed as she disengaged her arms to move away. "Your mother probably has her stopwatch set and is counting the minutes you've been here."

He raised his eyebrows and glanced worriedly toward the window. "You think so?"

"I was kidding. Don't look so worried." The man was really worried about this matchmaking business.

They left the brightness of the kitchen for the coziness of the living room, lit by a single lamp. Dillon look around, noticing the comfortable, yet nicely kept, furniture. It wasn't the white walls and chrome accents of his own home, but it was nice, clean and without a huge amount of clutter. A rag-eared teddy bear poked out from behind one cushion on the sofa and a pair of very small, mismatched shoes sat under the coffee table.

"You know, this is nice." Dillon looked around the room. "In fact, the whole house is nice. Three bedrooms?"

"You sound just like Jan," Jill said, laughing. "You know it has three bedrooms, it's almost identical to your mother's house."

"I thought it felt familiar. What do you use the extra bedroom for, a toy room for Penny?"

"Come look," she offered as she quietly led the way up the staircase located in one corner of the living room, mindful of the sleeping children. At the top of the stairs, Jill clicked on a light.

"I'm impressed," Dillon admitted as they stood in the brightly lit open space that formed the second story of Jill's home. It was furnished with an efficient work space, with a closed laptop sitting on the well-used desk. Two file cabinets adorned with plants stood in one corner and a window was framed by drapes, closed now against the night. Except for the large doll house in one corner, it was worthy of an office in any business in the country.

"You took out the closet," he commented as he walked around, touching an elephant figurine on a shelf and stopping to look at a painting on the wall.

"I really didn't need it and I like the extra space it gave me."

"I do too. Maybe I should suggest to Mom that she do her upstairs the same way. She said something about making it a guest bedroom or a sewing room."

"Speaking of your mother...."

"I know, I know, I'm going," Dillon muttered as they retraced their steps back to the living room. He didn't stop until they reached the front door. "One would almost think you're trying to get rid of me."

"Just trying to protect your reputation," Jill said, smiling.

"Isn't that supposed to be the other way around?" He drew her into his arms. "If we're going to protect my reputation then I'd better have my goodnight kiss before we open the door," he said, lowering his lips to hers.

By the time the kiss ended Jill had decided there was nothing she liked better than his kisses. Or maybe it was the man. Either way, she was feeling things she had never felt before. It was exhilarating.

"Jill?"

"Hmm?"

"I asked if it would be all right if I called you." Dillon patiently repeated his request. She had given him her number when plans were made for the circus date.

"Oh," she said. "Do you think that's wise?"

"Wise?"

"Yes you know, with your mother living next door and all. You don't want to end up married to me," Jill reminded him.

Didn't he? No, he didn't. Jill was right. "But she wouldn't know, would she?"

"I guess not," Jill reluctantly agreed. Unless Penny happened to be in the room, she thought. Penny was pretty nosy when it came to phone calls.

Why was she dragging her feet? Jill wondered later as she snuggled in bed, listening to the breeze rustling the leaves of the big oak tree outside her open window. Dillon Hanley was an attractive man and a good companion as well as a good sport. He sounded a bit like a dog. And attractive? The man had a monopoly on looks. But Ron had been attractive too, and look where that had gotten her. Of course, Dillon wasn't Ron, Jill reminded herself.

She just didn't want Dillon to get involved in a relationship he didn't want. No, that wasn't true, She didn't want to get involved in a relationship that had no chance of evolving into a lifetime commitment. She had liked being married, had liked having someone to come home to at the end of a long day and someone to share the day's news. Penny was a wonderful child and the best thing to come out of her marriage but she was no substitute for someone to confide in, to share her fears and joys.

There was Jan, she admitted. She had shared almost everything with Jan from the time she was born, but Jan had her own family now and Jill would never interfere in her sister's happiness by intruding on day-to-day basis.

Maybe Dillon wouldn't call her once he got back to his business and country-club routine. Today had been a fluke for him. He had gotten himself into a situation and saw it through but the day was over.

She punched her pillow. Why was she even worrying about it? She wasn't some teenager who was concerned about dates and boys, she was a woman with her own business, a child to raise and a full and happy life. If he called, that was fine, but if he didn't, it wasn't worth losing sleep over. And on that note, Jill was finally able to sleep.

Across town, Dillon was having a similar conversation with himself. Jill Baxter did strange and wonderful things to his system, he had to admit. Even now, just thinking about her finely shaped brows, her laughing mouth, those big brown eyes that a man could drown in, brought up emotions. And it wasn't that she was just gorgeous, because he could handle that. Maybe. She was one of the most sincere people he had ever met. She cared about the feelings of others, including his, someone she had only known a few hours.

Dillon knew she hadn't really been trying to get rid of him, her responses to his kisses told him that. She pushed him away at his own request. He had as good as told her he didn't want commitments and he didn't. Did he? No. He turned over his pillow. You're a basket case, he told himself, go to sleep.

****

It wasn't raining, Ruth Hanley thought as she looked out her living room window early Sunday afternoon. She had just finished washing her lunch dishes when she heard a vehicle drive up and stop in front of her home. No, it wasn't raining. It was a perfect Minnesota spring day, sunny and mild without much humidity. And it wasn't her birthday or a holiday, or any other special occasion. It was a perfect day for golfing and that's usually how Dillon spent his Sunday afternoons. As long as the weather wasn't bad, she knew where to find Dillon and his brother Jason. That's where they had spent most of their free time all their lives, tagging along with their father from the time they could walk and hold a golf club. Ruth always enjoyed the alone time that was Sunday afternoon. When they were done, they would all come back to the house for dinner.

And what was that he was getting out of his pickup? Flowers? Ruth removed her glasses and rubbed her eyes before putting them on again. She squinted. Yes, it was flowers. A whole box of them. What on Earth was the boy up to?

Penny saw him at the same time from next door.

"Mom," she yelled. "It's Dillon! It's Grandma Ruth's Dillon!"

"Here?" Jill muttered. Oh Lord, he said maybe he would call, not stop by. Jill grimaced as she look down at her old jeans and worn purple Mankato State University sweatshirt. Her hair was caught up in a messy bun with a purple scrunchy. She supposed she shouldn't really wear purple with her hair color, but she and Jan had decided years ago if they liked a color they should wear it.

"No, he's going to Grandma Ruth's. Rats." Penny turned from the window as Jill breathed a sigh of relief. After church she and Penny had eaten lunch and were headed out the door for the Kanowskys to make sure everything was in order for their return that evening from Florida. Jill had dusted the furniture earlier in the week, but wanted to get some fresh flowers as a welcome for the elderly couple who had given Jill and Penny so much support when they had first come to Mankato.

Later she and Penny were going to Jan's for a barbecue with her husband Grant, and Peggy, something they did almost every Sunday evening when the weather was nice. Occasionally,

Jill and Jan's parents would come down from Minneapolis to join them, as did the girls' brother Nance. Tonight, however, it would just be the two families and Jill knew that being comfortable was more important than being fashionable. Still, knowing Dillon Hanley was next door made her want to go back and change into something a little nicer. Forget it, Baxter, she told herself, he didn't come to see you, he's visiting his mother. He's not going to see what you're wearing.

Jill kept silently repeating that as she washed Penny's face and hands and helped her put on sandals. Today Jill had corralled Penny's unruly hair into braids.

"Can I go outside now?" Penny asked when Jill pronounced her ready.

"I suppose, but stay in the yard and don't get dirty," Jill said. "I'll be out in a minute."

Penny was out the door before Jill finished her sentence. She shook her head, then dashed to her room to change into a t-shirt. She gathered up her purse and keys, then remembered the salad in the refrigerator she had prepared for supper. By the time she got outside to the car, Penny was nowhere to be seen.

"Penny?" Jill put her things in the car. "Drat the kid, where is she now? Penny!"

"Over here Mom," Penny shouted. The little girl waved from her perch on the fence separating their lawn from Ruth's yard. "Come see what Dillon's doin.'"

Jill hesitated, not liking the way her body reacted to the mention of his name. She looked at her watch and sighed before heading for the fence. She was almost afraid to see what Dillon was doing since he wasn't visible from this side of the fence, but at least Penny was only watching.

"Look Mom, Dillon's plantin' flowers."

"He sure is." Jill peered over the fence to look at the brightly-colored marigolds, but got distracted by the broad muscles of Dillon's shoulders, pulling his shirt tight across his back. His hair was ruffled and he was wearing the same pair of paint-spattered jeans he was wearing the day before. She licked her lips, almost in involuntary anticipation.

Dillon chose that moment to look up. Jill blushed guiltily as his eyebrows rose.

"What do you think?"

"I think they're cool, what about you Mom?"

Jill had a sinking feeling he hadn't been talking about the flowers, but for a change was glad Penny interrupted the adult conversation. "Yes, they're very nice," she said, looking around. "Where's you mother?"

"She went to get some water for the flowers," Penny answered.

"Penny," Jill asked, pulling gently on her daughter's braid, "is it necessary to answer every question for us?"

Penny stuck out her bottom lip to pout for a moment, then brightened. "Can I help plant the flowers?"

"No, we need to get going and I don't want you to get all dirty," Jill replied. Because she would get dirty.

"Maybe next time," Dillon added.

"Hey, he could come with us, couldn't he, Mom?" Penny cocked her head to look back up at her mother. "Please?" She turned back to Dillon. "We're going to a barbecue, and have hot dogs. You want to come, don't cha'?"

"I really don't think..."

"Dillon probably has other plans..."

Both adults spoke at once.

"And Grandma Ruth, she could come too," Penny added. She jumped down from her perch and bounced up and down.

"Please, Mom, please?"

"Where could I go too?" Ruth asked, arriving on the scene with a large watering can. She was still bemused by Dillon's unexpected appearance on a Sunday afternoon.

"To a barbecue, with us, at Peggy's house," Penny answered.

"Jill?" Ruth looked at the other woman. In fact, everyone was looking at Jill and waiting for her decision, Penny with hopeful expectation, Ruth with concern and Dillon with a barely concealed grin. She decided to give in gracefully.

"Yes, yes, yes, I'm sure it will be fine if we bring guests," Jill said, smiling. She knew Jan would have no objections as she loved Ruth as much as Jill and Penny did. As far as Dillon went, well, it would make things interesting. "I'll call Jan once we get in the car and let her know."

"Wonderful. I'll make something to bring along," Ruth declared.

"Yay, yay," Penny squealed, jumping up and down.

"If you really mean it," Dillon added from his kneeling position on the grass.

"I do," Jill said, "but it's not until this evening. We usually eat around six. I'll text you the address."

"That's fine," Ruth replied, nodding her head. "That will give Dillon time to finish my flowers." Since he was actually here with them, Ruth was going to make sure she got them planted. She wanted to remember this day.

"We have to run over to the Kanowsky's this afternoon," Jill said, looking at her phone. "In fact, we should get going. Come on Penny. Ruth, Dillon, we'll see you tonight." They waved as they left the fence to go to the car, Penny bouncing along in front of Jill.

"Are you happy now?" Ruth asked her son as the Baxters drove away.

"Happy?"

"Yes, that you just finagled an invitation to spend the evening with my next-door neighbor."

"Hey, I didn't finagle anything. I hardly said a word," Dillon defended himself. "You were the one who accepted for us. I don't even know where we're going for this barbecue."

"Well, to Jan and Grant Humphrey's, of course, that's where Jill and Penny spend every Sunday evening."

"You've been to one of these before?" Dillon was beginning to think he didn't know his mother. He always thought he and his brother Jason knew everything their mother did, but right now it didn't look that way.

"As a matter of fact, yes, they invited me over just after I moved here," Ruth replied, moving beside him to water the freshly planted flowers. "They're very informal and Jill and Jan are just sweethearts. They've always made me feel at home."

Dillon wasn't sure why, but he was a little jealous. He admitted he and Jason spent much of their free time on the golf course but so had their parents. Come to think of it, only since Alvin Hanley had died the previous year had Ruth quit golfing completely. She hadn't golfed much with the boys but would often join the three of them when they went. Dillon hadn't noticed that before, but now that he had, he intended to discover why. And why she seemed less than pleased that he was tagging along tonight. After all, she was the matchmaker here. He figured she would want him to spend time with the wonderful Jill Baxter, who must have some faults, but at the moment he couldn't come up with any. Maybe spending more time with her would help him find those.

"Mom?"

"Yes, dear?"

"Why don't you golf anymore?"

Ruth considered the question as they began gathering up the gardening tools and finally shrugged.

"I don't know, I guess I've outgrown it." Ruth smiled sadly as they walked around the house and into the kitchen. She missed her husband and now that he was gone, golfing wasn't the same. "I've got other things to do now that I'm responsible for my own house," she added as Dillon washed up at the sink. She laughed as she held up the hand sporting a hard plastic brace. "And, you have to admit, playing golf with this thing on would be more of a handicap that the pros would be willing to give me."

Dillon didn't believe her explanation for a minute but let the subject drop as he made arrangements to pick Ruth up that evening for the ride to the Humphreys. Maybe he would tackle his brother about it when he saw him. Jason always seemed to know what their mother was up to. In the meantime, maybe he could further his relationship with Jill. He realized he was probably playing right into his mother's plans, but Jill said she wasn't interested in marriage, so there wasn't any reason they couldn't have a good time together. A backyard barbecue might be a nice change from the country club. He had enjoyed the circus, after all.

****

When the third mosquito bit him on the neck, Dillon decided there was something to be said for country clubs, especially those that were regularly sprayed for pesky flying insects. He was sitting in a lawn chair on Jan and Grant's patio nursing a beer and discussing the Twins' baseball season with Grant, a big bear of a man who used to play professional football and now coached at Mankato State University. He looked much like Dillon had pictured Jill's husband to look like, only he had streaks of gray in his dark hair and was missing the pot belly. Dillon decided Grant Humphrey was not a person to meet in a dark alley, but he was pleasant enough company in the daylight.

Dillon looked around. The view from the Humphrey's home was amazing. The house sat on a bluff overlooking the town and the Minnesota River. Located not far from the college, the house was comfortable. It was mid-century in design, with open rooms and lots of glass. The view was visible from almost everywhere in the home. The patio was paved with native rock and the open fencing made it a perfect place for a Sunday night get-together.

All those gathered in the Humphrey backyard were good company, Dillon reflected. His gaze followed Jill's lithe body as she and the other girls played soccer with a large multi-colored ball. His mother was trying to clap and cheering them on. She appeared to be having a wonderful time. He frowned, wondering at the change in her when she was with this family. He had always thought of his mother as prim, always dressed for company and every hair in place. Tonight she was wearing leggings and a pullover top that came down to mid-thigh.

His gaze went back to Jill. At least he thought she was Jill. They were dressed the same this evening in jeans and white t-shirts, and impossible to tell apart. He wondered idly if they called each other every day before deciding what to wear.

He voiced this thought to Grant, who laughed. "I used to think so too when I was dating Jan. Then I discovered they have a sort of telepathy with each other. They just pick out the same clothes. So do Penny and Peggy."

"Whew! Talk about your identical twins," Dillon commented. "How on earth do you tell them apart?" he asked Grant.

Grant laughed again. "Trust me, I can tell. And besides, they aren't really identical. They aren't even twins. Jan's a year older than Jill."

Dillon's eyes widened, then he remembered. "I guess Jan told me that yesterday, but I was, ah, distracted right then. But you can't tell they're not twins."

"Not from this distance, but you can tell them apart," Grant said. "Jill has more lines on her face, thanks to Ron Baxter, her ex-husband, and is now just starting to gain back her self-confidence. She took quite a hit to her esteem when he left her.

"You can see the difference in their stances. They also smell different but that's harder to notice and even harder to explain." The big man shrugged. "Maybe you have to be in love with one of them to tell the difference."

Dillon wasn't in love, but he watched them closely, trying to spot any difference in the way the two women moved. He finally settled his gaze on Jill as she kicked the ball. At least he thought it was Jill.

She wished he would stop staring at her, it was making her nervous, Jill thought as she tried to kick the ball to Peggy. She was surprised he actually came. Ruth was always welcome, but as Jill had confided earlier to her sister, Dillon didn't seem the type to be happy sitting watching a four-person soccer game and drinking beer. Still, for some reason, Jill was happy he came. It was nice not to be the lone man, or woman, out, for once. He had treated her casually all evening, yet he seemed to be watching her all the time. She wondered briefly if her zipper was open.

They had all laughed at the antics of the young girls as they tried to contend with their first slices of watermelon. Always before they had eaten it cut up in bite-sized pieces. And Dillon watched her. The men had helped clean up from supper, and

Dillon never even brushed up against Jill. But he watched her. Jill shivered as she recalled the promise of his gaze each time she looked at him and caught him watching her.

Penny caught the ball with her legs and kicked it by Jan and Peggy into an imaginary goal. "Yay, we win, we win!"

"That's enough for these old bones," Jan declared, collapsing on the grass.

"Mine too," Jill added as she helped her sister up. The three women walked back to the patio and the comfort of padded patio chairs. Peggy and Penny went to play on the playset, located in the corner of the fenced-in yard.

"I thought the Kanowskys would be back by now," Jill mused as the adults enjoyed the coolness of the darkening evening. They were supposed to be back that afternoon, but she hadn't heard from them. Their car wasn't in their drive.

"Don't worry about Edna and George," Jan advised her sister. "They drove this trip and you know George loves to stop at every tourist place they can find. It wouldn't surprise me if they are still somewhere in the Ozarks."

"The Ozarks?" Ruth asked. "I always thought I would like to see the Ozarks. Alvin and I never seemed to get away much."

Jill and Jan exchanged looks as Jill explained that George and Edna always spent the winters in Florida but liked to take their time as they returned home. This wasn't the first time the older woman had mentioned things she would like to do. Jill and Jan had discussed that Ruth might be lonely, and decided that once George and Edna got back, they would introduce her to one of their friends, do a little matchmaking of their own. Jill smiled at the thought and looked up to see Dillon watching her. Again. She rose from the chair.

"Um, I think maybe Penny and I should be getting home.

It looks like someone's going to need a bath before she goes to bed," she said, looking pointedly at Penny.

Dillon rose as well, taking Jill's cue.

"Grant, it was nice meeting you," he said, shaking the other man's hand. "Maybe we'll run into each other sometime. Keep up the good work with the football team." He turned to his mother as Grant nodded. "Mom, are you ready to go?"

"I sure am. Jan, you be sure and let me know when you need me to watch Peggy this week, I'll be happy to do it," Ruth said, gathering her purse and jacket.

In a flurry of activity the guests cleared off the patio and headed towards their respective vehicles for the trip across town. Jan and Grant lived in the newer part of the city and had a wonderful view, but Jill preferred her little bungalow in the original part of Mankato. Of course, if she ever wanted to admire the view, all she had to do was visit Jan or the Kanowskys.

"Can I ride with Dillon and Grandma Ruth, Mom?" Penny tugged on Jill's arm.

"I think you have to ask Dillon that, sweetie."

Please, can I Dillon, can I?" Penny shouted, bouncing over to Dillon.

"That depends," Dillon knelt down to her level. He was getting smarter, he decided, and was going to find out what he was getting into before he agreed to anything. "What do you want to do?"

"Ride with you and Grandma Ruth. Can I?"

Dillon ruffled her fair. "Sure you can."

"Can I sit in the front seat with you?" was the next question.

"Penny, you know the rules," Jill interrupted. "Car seat, in the back seat."

Penny was disappointed, but at least she tried.

"Jill, why don't I ride with you?" Ruth asked.

Dillon stopped. They were going to leave him alone with a child? He didn't think that was a good idea. He looked at Jill, then his mother, and lastly, at Penny and silently conceded he had been conned again.

Jill finished moving the car seat from her SUV to Dillon's pickup and strapped Penny in. She gave her daughter a kiss and backed away, waving at both of them.

Dillon shrugged and got in the pickup. Why did he always feel like he was in the twilight zone and had no control over anything when this child and her mother were around?

As she and Ruth drove down the winding road, Jill could see the headlights of Dillon's pickup in the rear view mirror. She laughed quietly at the thought of Dillon Hanley cruising around town with a six-year-old for a passenger.

"What?" Ruth turned to see why Jill was laughing about.

"Just thinking about your son."

Ruth didn't say anything but nodded in agreement.

"What's that mean?" Jill couldn't resist asking, laughing.

"Nothing, nothing at all."

"Well, you have to admit, he can be amusing."

"Oh, I'll admit it all right." Ruth paused for a moment, then continued. "Do you like him?"

"You're as bad as he is," Jill replied before she thought.

Ruth's raised eyebrows in the dimness of the car caught the corner of Jill's eye. "Yes, he can be pleasant company and I did enjoy the circus last night. The girls like him and despite the fact he says he doesn't like kids, he seems to be a good sport."

"Hmm..."

"Now don't get any ideas."

"I'm not," Ruth assured her. "I tried to tell him I wasn't trying to get you two together. I didn't invite him over today and

I wasn't the one who invited him to this barbecue."

"I know" Jill groaned. "I was surprised when he accepted Penny's invitation."

"Me too," Ruth agreed. "And imagine my surprise this afternoon when he showed up with those flowers. He hasn't missed a Sunday afternoon of golf for as long as I can remember, except when the weather's been bad."

She watched out the window for a few moments before continuing. "I have to admit I wouldn't mind having you as a daughter-in-law, especially if it's a choice between you and some hoity-toity woman who couldn't do anything in case she broke a nail, but I'm not going to interfere in his life."

Jill patted her hand. "I know and you wouldn't interfere in mine either." She sighed. "Between you and me, I think Dillon would make a wonderful husband and father. But we both know he's not interested in marriage."

"We'll see," was all the older woman would say and Jill didn't get a chance to ask anything else as she pulled into the driveway and Ruth got out.

Dillon pulled in behind them and Penny bounced out of the pickup, jumping down to the pavement.

"How was the ride, sweetie?" Jill asked her daughter.

"It was fun, Mom, but he wouldn't go as fast as I wanted." Penny pushed her bottom lip out into a pout.

"That's because I was ahead of you and we were going fast enough, young lady. Now into the house for a bath," Jill told her. They bid the Hanleys goodnight and Jill thanked Dillon for allowing Penny to ride with him. Ruth started walking toward her house but Dillon held back.

"I enjoyed Penny's company on the way here," he said. It sounded lame to him.

Jill laughed, surprised to hear him say it. "Even if she does talk all the time," Jill finished for him. His grin told her he was thinking the same thing. "Well, goodnight, Dillon." She turned away. It was awkward.

Dillon cleared his throat. "Um, Jill?"

"Yes?" She turned around.

"Would you like to have dinner one night this week?'

"Dinner?"

"Yes, you know, that meal in the evening?"

She smiled. "I know what it is, but what about your mother?"

"I can leave her at home."

"That's not what I meant."

He laughed. "Look, I had a talk with my mother this afternoon and I made it clear we weren't interested in each other."

He crossed his fingers behind his back as he had seen her do on occasions when she didn't want to say the entire truth, hoping Jill wouldn't question his statement. Because he was interested in her. Every inch of her. Maybe if he spent more time with her and discovered a few of her faults, he could get her out of his system. And if their physical attraction led to other things, then so be it.

"That's right," Jill agreed. She crossed her fingers hoping he wouldn't see. "So why go out on a date? We don't want to give your mother the wrong idea."

"Trust me," Dillon said. "I know what I'm doing."

Chapter 4

Did he really know what he was doing? Probably not, Dillon decided as he got ready for Friday night's date with Jill. Mother or no mother, he was in trouble. He claimed he didn't want marriage, even with someone like Jill Baxter, yet he had gone against his better judgment and asked her on a date. Trust me, he told her. He wasn't even sure he trusted himself.

Because he wanted Jill. He couldn't lie to himself about that. His stomach had been doing somersaults all week every time he thought of her, and that was most of the time.

Every time the phone rang or someone knocked on his office door, Dillon's stomach tightened in anticipation. Why she would come to his office Dillon had no idea, but he hoped she would. He had to stop himself several times from going over to see his mother after work, telling himself she would get suspicious and figure out he just wanted to be closer to her neighbor. And it wasn't just physical, he finally admitted to himself.

He wanted to get to know her, laugh with her, understand her feelings. He was certain she hadn't told many people about her husband and was surprised she told him. She must have been devastated when he left her and her newborn daughter and yet she had survived. Yep, he wanted to get to know her better.

Well, part of it was physical, he admitted as he knocked on Jill's door a little while later. Definitely physical, he decided as she opened the door and greeted him. She was wearing a slate blue dress that clung in all the right places and swung gracefully when she walked. She had her hair in a fancy braid pinned to the back of her head and looked cool and elegant as she went to get her purse and phone. He forced his brain to tell his body to behave as Penny bounded through the kitchen door.

"Whoa," he laughed as she ran into his legs. "Don't you ever just walk?" Penny shook her head as Dillon bent down to her level to give her a hug. Two weeks ago he would never have considered hugging a little girl. He didn't even give hugs to his own nephew.

"What'cha doin' here?" Penny asked, peering up at him as he straightened up.

"Penny," he mother admonished, "I told you Dillon and I were going out to dinner tonight."

"Oh yeah," she replied. "Did you know today was my last day of school?" She raised her arms in a victory salute. "It's summer now."

Dillon raised his eyebrows. "Is it?" he asked and she nodded. "That's exciting. What are you going to do all summer?"

Penny thought about it for a moment. "Play with my toys," she replied. "Do you want to stay here and play with me? I have lots of toys." She pushed her bottom lip out into an adorable pout.

It almost worked. "Maybe another time," Dillon promised. "After all, you have all summer free."

"Okay. You want to see my room?"

"We need to get going, Penny," Jill interrupted, "and Dillon has already seen your room, when he brought us home from the circus remember? Why don't you run and wash your hands so you can have your own dinner?" Jill suggested.

Penny gave Dillon's legs another hug, then ran off

in the direction of the kitchen, leaving the door swing-ing.

Dillon looked up as the door swung back out and Penny bounded back into the room, with a woman he knew well.

"Mother?" He was confused.

"Why, hello Dillon." She stepped closer to give him a kiss on the cheek. "I didn't expect to see you here," Ruth said. "Oh, I suppose you tried to find me at my house. Well I'm babysitting tonight with Penny so Jill can go out."

Dillon reached to pick up Penny, like he did it all the time. "Well, um, actually, I'm taking Jill out for din-ner."

"You are?" Ruth's eyebrows rose behind her glass-es.

"Oh yes, Ruth, didn't I tell you that?" Jill asked with a smile as she entered the room.

"Oh, maybe you did, I must have forgotten," Ruth answered. "Well, you two have a good time," she added as Dillon sat Penny on her feet on the floor. She ushered the couple to the door. "We have lots of things to do, don't we Penny?"

"Yep, we're going to make cookies after supper. We'll save some for you guys," Penny answered.

"You had better save more than some, little girl," Jill advised, giving her daughter a hug. "Have fun now and go to bed when Ruth says it's time."

****

"You never told my mother you were going out with me tonight, did you?" Dillon asked as they pulled up to the Blue Earth restaurant on Walnut Street in historic downtown Mankato, one of several unique restaurants on the area. He was driving his car, a sporty little BMW. The pickup was fine for work and served him well in the winter, but he loved this car and drove it whenever possible.

Jill ran her hand across the dash. It was a beautiful car. It wasn't necessarily practical for a woman with a child but it was nice. It fitted Dillon.

Dillon parked in front of the restaurant. Somehow the country club didn't feel right for Jill. He wanted something a little more intimate, where they could get to know one another better. Never mind that the chances were pretty good that Suzanne would be at the club. That's where she and the rest of Dillon's friends, Dillon included, spent most Fridays night.

"Of course not," Jill answered breezily, bringing him back to the present and the question at hand. "I didn't want her to think we were serious about each other, that we're dating. That may have gone out the window though when I asked her to watch Penny while I was out. I completely overlooked the fact that she would see you when you came to pick me up."

"But we are dating." Dillon thumped his palm on the steering wheel. "We're going out to dinner, I picked you up at your house, so it's a date."

"Okay, don't get mad. It's a date, but it's not a serious relationship. So why didn't you tell your mother we were going out? You're the one who said 'trust me.'"

"Why did you ask her to babysit? Don't you know any

teenagers?" He ignored her last comment. He had decided a long time ago that he didn't know what he was talking about when he said that.

"Yes, I do, but Penny adores your mother and your mother likes the company She's lonely," Jill retorted as Dillon unsnapped his seat belt and got out of the car to walk around to the passenger's side.

The restaurant was housed in what used to be an abandoned Art Deco building. The outside of the building retained its history and the restaurant was cozy and comfortable. It was part of historic downtown Mankato and Jill thought they had amazing food.

It was probably a good thing they were there, Jill thought, because she was on the verge of shouting at him for not listening to her and she truly preferred not to argue.

To Jill's relief they weren't able to continue the discussion as they entered the restaurant that featured leather booths and warm lighting. Blue Earth was one of Jill's favorite places to eat and she was happy Dillon had chosen it.

She had been afraid they would end up going to the country club and had a hard time picturing herself there. Just the thought of herself in golf clothes and riding around in one of these little carts or sipping cocktails in the lounge was enough to make Jill smile as Dillon ordered them a bottle of wine.

"You're beautiful when you smile," he commented as the waiter left.

Jill raised her eyebrows. "Are you saying I'm ugly when I'm not?" Jill opened the menu although she already knew what she was ordering. The pesto salmon was the best Jill had ever tasted and with a salad it made the perfect meal.

"No, of course not," Dillon stated before he realized she was teasing him. "You're beautiful all the time."

"That's better then." Jill nodded in agreement.

"I walked right into that, didn't I?"

"Sure did. Have you decided what you're going to have?' She was laughing now and he joined her.

As predicted, her dinner was perfect and Dillon enjoyed his steak as well. They chatted about the latest movies and books that interested them and discovered they shared an interest in a variety of topics. Dillon revealed that for all of his strait-laced banker talk and clothes, he loved books about pirates, from Treasure Island to paperback romances, as long as pirates were involved.

Jill admitted she enjoyed reading the Wall Street Journal, even if no one except Penny and Jan knew it.

They discussed going to Minneapolis to see a Broadway production but decided their own community offered many of the same cultural opportunities.

They were finishing their wine and listening to the soft background music when a movement caught Jill's eye. It was the Hendricksens. Mary was waving at her. Jill groaned.

Dillon turned to see caught her attention, then groaned as well. Mary and Ted were headed their way.

"Well, what do you know?" Mary said, looking at Jill. "This is a surprise, seeing you out twice in one week. We didn't know you were seeing anyone." She raised her eyebrows and waited for a reply.

"Well," Jill said, trying not to stutter. "You remember Dillon Hanley? His mother is my next-door neighbor."

"I remember," Mary replied. "Did she come with you?" She looked around.

Jill wanted to slide under the table. "No, she's watching Penny tonight," she said.

"I see," Mary said. She was distracted by her husband pulling on her arm.

"Now, Mary," he said. "I believe the hostess is waiting to seat us. Come along and leave these two be."

Dillon could have hugged the man, he thought as the couple walked away, with Mary taking several glances back at the two of them.

"Well, that was awkward," he said.

Jill laughed. "It was," she said. "I thought you were going to have a heart attack. I take it you're not used to seeing people you know?"

Dillon shook his head. "I run into people I know all the time," he said. "It's an occupational hazard. I'm just not usually made to feel like I'm stealing cookies from a cookie jar."

"She is something, isn't she?" Jill answered. "But she doesn't mean any harm. I suspect it's more about me being out and about and with a man to boot that has her curiosity aroused. I'm not sure she's ever seen me in public with a man."

Dillon digested that information. "You don't date much, do you?" he asked. It surprised him when Jill shook her head.

"I spend a lot of time with Jan, and Penny and I do tons of things together. But most people, like Mary and Ted, know us from Penny's school activities. I usually go to those alone, so I can see where she might be surprised to see me out with a man."

They fell quiet and both wondered what to say next.

"You know, you never answered my question about my mother watching Penny," Dillon commented as picked up his glass of wine. He decided bringing the conversation back to his mother would keep his mind on safer subjects than nosy friends and the way Jill's scent drifted to him across the table. Or the way her lips framed her perfect smile when she was teasing him. Stop it, Hanley, he told himself, you'll be drooling over her in a moment. Listen to her, she's talking to you, he lectured himself. Pay attention to what she's saying instead of how she smells.

"I thought I did."

"Did what?" Dillon was still arguing with his body.

"Answer your question," Jill replied. "Are you even listening to me?" She raised an eyebrow.

"Yes, of course I am. What else would I be doing?" he asked, taking a sip of his drink to cover his blunder. "And no, you didn't answer my question."

Jill considered for a moment. It really wasn't her business to discuss Ruth with her son. On the other hand, maybe he should know how lonely his mother was without her husband.

"All right," she said. "The real reason I got your mother to babysit for Penny was because she asked if she could."

"She asked to babysit? I don't believe it." Dillon was incredulous. "She doesn't even babysit much for Jason and Meredith and Ben is her grandson."

"Do they ask her?" Jill asked.

"I don't know," he replied. "I guess I just assumed they did and she said no."

"As a matter of fact, she loves kids," Jill said. "If you

ever stopped by her house during the week, when she knows you won't, you would probably see two or three there at one time or another, sampling her cookies, helping her in the yard, walking with her to the store so they can help carry groceries home." She leaned forward, warming to her topic. "She's lonely and the kids on the block know it as well as I do. Penny's even talked about fixing her up with a neighbor from down the block."

"A six-year-old wants to fix her up with a man? My mother?"

Jill ignored the questions as her mind worked furiously. "Now that I think about it, there's this friend of the Kanwoskys. He wouldn't be too bad. He's widowed and about her age. Maybe..."

"Now, don't you start matchmaking Jill," Dillon warned. "She's my mother and she isn't lonely. She and my dad had lots of friends. They played golf and bridge and..."

"Your father played golf and you boys played golf," Jill said softly. "Your father is gone now and so are you boys. She's still a woman, Dillon, not just your mother," she reminded him gently. "Think about it."

He wasn't looking very happy, Jill decided, but she was glad she said something. Ruth was a dear lady and deserved to be happy during this chapter of her life. Jill took a last sip of her wine.

The silence between them was deafening.

"You know, there's a live band playing at a place down the street," Dillon finally ventured. He didn't agree with her but he had asked her. "Would you like to take a walk and check it out?"

Jill did, so Dillon paid the bill and they walked out

into the cool night. It was a great night for a walk, Jill thought.

They could hear music playing as they got closer, it resonated out into the street. Hucklebee's was a great place for live music. Tonight's band was playing 1940's swing band music but the place was packed when they entered.

They made their way through the crowd and found a free table. They ordered glasses of wine and when the music slowed, stepped out onto the dance floor. Surprisingly, many of the couples on the dance floor were in their thirties.

"It's nice to do something besides argue with each other," Dillon said, smiling as he led her onto the smooth wooden floor. "After all, it is our first date."

He took her in his arms to glide slowly around the floor staying in time with the old melody the band was playing.

"Makes dancing worthwhile again," he murmured against her neck. He and Jill were the exact same height, something Dillon found much more satisfying than a nose stuck in his shoulder when he danced with someone shorter.

"What does?" Jill was afraid she had missed the gist of the conversation while she was savoring the feel of his hand on the small of her back, the other gently holding her own.

"The absence of hard rock, hip hop, rap. All of it," he said. "I think I've just discovered why all those older people resisted rock and roll. It wasn't because of the music, it was because they didn't have an excuse to dance close anymore."

"You might be right," Jill murmured as she enjoyed the feel of his hard body against her own swaying gently with the music. The danced to several songs until the band picked up the beat and moved into a faster song.

It was probably a good time to stop dancing, Jill decided as they moved back to their table. They had been barely moving, yet she was breathless. A few more minutes out on the floor and she would have melted into a pool of feminine awareness right there. When Dillon suggested they leave, Jill readily agreed. All she wanted was to go some place where they could be alone, undress him one button at a time and explore the body she had already felt so close to her own.

Sinful, she told herself as Dillon pulled the car away from the curb. You aren't a school girl with a crush on the football hero, you're a grown woman with a small child at home. Still, the thought of all that flesh exposed to her wandering hands, her lips chasing, gave her a thrill of anticipation. Unconsciously, Jill let her hand slide across the console of the car to rest on his thigh, the muscles of which flexed every time he put on the brakes.

Dillon cleared his throat."Um, where to now?"

His voice reminded Jill where they were. She looked down at her hand and pulled it back. "Oh, um well....it's been a long time since I dated. Where do you usually go on your dates?"

"My place," he said, grinning. "Great idea, since my mother's at your house." He headed his car in the proper direction. "This is great. I've never been able to use that excuse before."

"What excuse?"

"That we had to go to my place since my mother was

babysitting for my date," he replied.

Jill was still trying to figure out when she had agreed to go to his house.

"This doesn't sound good, Hanley," Jill finally managed. "All of the women you date go home with you? Just how many dates have you taken to your place?"

"I see what you mean. Okay," he amended, "only the ones I'm really interested in go home with me." He would never admit it, but he had never taken a woman to his home. He thought it sent the wrong message.

"That doesn't sound much better," she warned.

"How about... Maybe I should quit while I'm ahead," Dillon decided, glancing at the woman beside him. She didn't look like she was teasing this time.

"Maybe you should quit before I smack you."

"That too." He grinned. "Would you rather go somewhere else? I would hate to take you home at," he looked at the clock on the dashboard, "ten-fifteen. We may as well make it look good since my mother already knows I'm out with you."

"That's not very flattering either," Jill said, laughing. "Want to try for three in a row?"

"I think I'll stay at two," Dillon answered, joining her in laughter.

"And I think I would really like to see how a rich, single banker lives, so I say we go have a look at this den of inequity."

"That's good, because we're here," Dillon said as he pulled up to a garage attached to a townhouse complex. He gently picked up Jill's hand and smoothed his fingers over hers.

"And I wouldn't exactly call it a den of iniquity. I'll

have you know I have never iniquitized any dens here." He lifted her hand to his lips and brushed them against her palm, sensuously tasting the warmth of her. He heard her quick intake of breath as he did so.

Jill curled her hand shut and opened her door with the other hand, almost tripping in her haste to get out of the car because the small car was suddenly too confining. She took several deep breaths as she tried to steady her emotions. Dillon, acting like nothing had happened between them, guided her up the sidewalk and into his home. He pressed a light switch and Jill was able to look around.

What first impressed her was the simplicity of the design, clean lines and openness. The main room was decorated in white and dark blue with an island separating it from the kitchen area. Accents in chrome brought the space to life. She could see a lighted courtyard with a swimming pool centered in it through a patio door in the main room.

As she looked closer, Jill discovered it also looked lived in. Several photographs of his family were scattered around on the small tables at the ends of the sofa and several magazines littered the coffee table.

Dillon moved into the room, removed his sports jacket and rolled back the sleeves of his shirt, revealing the tanned skin of his forearms.

"Come in, make yourself comfortable."

"Said the spider to the fly," Jill muttered under her breath. It probably was an apt statement. And why shouldn't it be? She hadn't offered much resistance when he kissed her the first night, and certainly hadn't made him take her home when he mentioned coming here. So why was she feeling jittery all of a sudden? She looked down at her hand, which was still clenched, and told herself to relax.

After all, Dillon had said earlier that he was interested in her, hadn't he? He didn't want a serious relationship. Well, maybe she didn't either, she told herself. And it had been six long years since she had been sexually involved with anyone. Longer than that if she counted the months she was pregnant and she and Ron retreated from physical intimacy.

Maybe it was time for a nice, casual relationship with some good old-fashioned sex thrown in. Yes, that's what she needed. To heck with commitment, she was ready for some fun. Now that she had made her decision, Jill relaxed.

"What?" Dillon was looking at her questioningly. He had seen the changes of expression on her face and wondered what she was thinking.

"Oh, nothing." She moved over to the sofa and he followed. "You did say you were interested in me, didn't you?"

The question startled Dillon and he stood up again just as they had started to sit. What kind of question was that to ask? Of course he was interested, otherwise they wouldn't be here. What was she up to? He ran his finger around his collar, which was suddenly too tight. The phrase "marriage trap" popped into his mind.

"Um, yes, I guess I did," he replied as he moved into the kitchen. He loosened his tie and unbuttoned the top buttons on his shirt as he rummaged around in the cupboard for glasses. "Would you like something to drink?"

Jill decided he wasn't going to come sit with her, so

she rose and followed him into the kitchen.

"No thanks," she replied to his back as he turned to the refrigerator and filled his glass with ice and water from the dispenser. She placed her hands on his shoulders and ran them down the taut material of his shirt.

Dillon froze.

"What are you doing?"

"Nervous?" she questioned softly.

"Me? Nervous?" He turned around, barely daring to breathe, and edged out of Jill's grasp, setting the glass on the counter. She leaned against the refrigerator with a smile on her face.

"You forgot your glass," she commented as Dillon as she carried it to him. Dillon looked at the glass and then at her. She handed it to him and he took a long drink, swallowed wrong and began to cough.

Jill pounded him on the back.

"Enough!" he finally got out in between coughs. His eyes were watering and he was turning an unhealthy color of red. "I'm dying and you're not helping matters at all."

"Sorry," she said, helping him back to the sofa. "How about some water?" She went back to the kitchen, refilled his glass with water and carried it back. He was stretched out on the sofa with his arm over his eyes.

"Here's a new glass of water," she said. "Try not to drink it so fast."

He didn't answer.

"Are you all right?" Jill asked him, settling herself on the edge of the sofa.

"That depends." Dillon uncovered his face and opened one eye. "Are you going to try to kill me again?"

"Hey, I was just trying to help."

"You were trying to seduce me," he accused.

"And that's never happened before?"

"No, I mean, I'm the one who usually makes the first move," he amended as Jill's eyebrows rose. He swung his feet around and sat up, feeling foolish. "You just caught me by surprise."

"And are you feeling prepared now?" She leaned toward him and unbuttoned the next button on his shirt. He put his hand over hers to stop her and cleared his throat.

"You know, every time you get nervous, you clear your throat," Jill calmly observed.

"I'm not nervous," he almost shouted.

"What do you call it then? Are you shy?" She smiled and disengaged her hand. She moved it down to the next button. "Surely this town's biggest playboy isn't shy."

"That's enough," he ground out as he took her by the shoulders. Jill was the surprised one as he took her mouth. She quickly relaxed and enjoyed it, wondering why she hadn't done it this way to start. Her hands continued their downward trek until Dillon's shirt was pulled from his slacks and the last button was open to allow her fingers access to the warm flesh beneath.

"Oh, Jill, do you know what you're doing to me?" he murmured against her throat as he explored the curves and hollows there with his lips, down to where the neckline of her dress concealed more enticing secrets.

"I hope it's the same thing you're doing to me," Jill offered softly, bringing her hands around to his back to caress the muscles there. She lifted her lips to meet his again.

They were both as breathless as their first kiss had left them when Dillon finally pulled away. "You feel so good," he whispered into her hair.

Jill moved one of her hands so it rested and caressed the material of his slacks covering his arousal.

"We shouldn't be doing this," he got out between kisses.

Jill smiled at his choice of words. "Isn't that my line?"

"What?" He had gotten distracted by an earlobe that was just begging to be nibbled on.

"Last week I was the one saying we shouldn't be doing this. But then there was the possibility of interruption. Why shouldn't we be doing this tonight?"

"We've only known each other for a week," Dillon pointed out as he smoothed the soft material of her dress down off of her shoulders, seeking the wonders he knew he would find beneath.

"And you were shouting that you would only take me to the circus, never marry me."

For the second time that evening, Dillon froze. Marry? Why did that word keep coming up? She wasn't expecting marriage if they went to bed together, was she? No, of course not. And he certainly wasn't. So what was the problem?

"Dillon?"

Her voice brought him back to the present.

"What's wrong?"

He moved away from her and stood up, running his fingers through his hair.

"This isn't right," he said, pacing the floor. "We can't get involved like this."

"What are you talking about?" Jill pulled up her dress

and smoothed it down, aware the mood was gone. "And would you stop pacing? You're making me nervous."

He stopped and looked at her, then picked up his water and took a large gulp. Jill stayed seated on the sofa, silent.

What had she said? Something about the circus and him not wanting marriage. That's it, Jill realized, the comment about marriage had spooked him. Again.

She rose to go to him. "Look, Dillon, I never meant..."

"Just stay over there," he warned. "You know what happens every time we get too close to each other."

Jill stopped. "But Dillon, I told you I don't want to get married. Is there any reason we can't just enjoy each other?" And by that she meant what they were doing moments earlier.

Dillon didn't answer. He avoided her gaze. He wasn't sure what he wanted. She was making him crazy.

"Well then, maybe you should take me home."

"Maybe that would be best," Dillon agreed as he buttoned his shirt and tucked it into his slacks. He practically pushed her out the door and to the car. He needed to think. He didn't want marriage, he never considered marriage. He didn't want to have an affair with her either. He only knew he wanted to be with her. He wanted to attend family picnics with her and Penny and read the little girl bedtime stories. He wanted to hold Jill all night, every night. He wanted...well, he wasn't exactly sure, but it wasn't just a physical relationship, he was sure of it.

Neither said a word until they pulled up in front of Jill's house, but the tension in the car was almost palpable. Jill could see the way his knuckles gripped the steering wheel in the dimness of the car.

She went over and over the bizarre conversation they had just had. And it all came down to the same thing. Marriage.

They were both stiff and silent as they approached the front porch.

"I promise, Dillon, I'm not asking for marriage," Jill said softly as she paused with her hand on the door knob. The only light was from the porch light and it cast a soft shadow on their features.

"And dammit, Jill, I don't want an affair with you," he hissed. The door opened and his mother stuck her head out, startling them both.

"I thought I heard voices out here."

"It's just us Ruth," Jill replied as she entered, ignoring Dillon. She didn't want him to see the sadness in her eyes. "I hope we didn't worry you."

"Of course not, I just wasn't expecting you this soon." She looked at her son, who had stopped at the threshold and was scowling as Jill kicked off her shoes and placed her purse on the sofa. "I guess I won't ask if you had a good time."

"Come on Mom, I'll walk you home," Dillon told her. He ignored Jill's scathing look.

Ruth looked from one to the other, hopes of having Jill as a daughter fading. "Oh my. Well, yes, that would be nice." She gathered her sweater and hugged Jill goodnight, whispering, "it's his father's fault," to her.

Jill's resulting smile made Dillon even stiffer as he told her goodnight as well, before turning and escorting his mother out the door.

Jill automatically turned off lights and locked the door before going to her room, her heart heavy and her self-esteem in shreds. And as she lay in bed, only one thought went through her head. Over and over.

Chapter 5

Dammit, Jill, I don't want to have an affair with you.

Jill heard the words over and over as she stared at the ceiling in her bedroom, watching the design made there by the slight sway of the tree outside. He didn't want marriage, and now he didn't even want an affair. But Jill was sure he wanted her, or he had at one point, his arousal had assured her of that. So why had he stopped? The joke she made about marrying her. Okay, that made sense, but she said an affair would be fine with her.

Dammit, Jill, I don't want to have an affair with you.

So she was back where she started, confused. She punched her pillow. This was the second time she had trouble getting to sleep since meeting Dillon Hanley. And the man didn't deserve this much thought. So what if he was a hunk, and fun to be with and a good sport? So what? So what if he made her feel things she never felt before? They just weren't compatible, and that was that.

She just was having bad luck with men, Jill told herself. With Ron, Jill had been comfortable, after all, they had known each other for years. Look what he had done to her. And now, finally she had gotten her self-confidence back. She finds a man she could be interested in and what happens? He decides that she's not what he wants. He can't even handle an affair with her. Jill turned over again. The man was making her crazy.

****

"Crazy, huh?" Jan relaxed on her lounger. She and Jill

were enjoying the sunshine on Jan's patio Saturday afternoon. The Minnesota winters were cold, but the mild weather of late spring more than made up for it. It was warm without being hot. A gentle breeze rustled the new leaves of nearby trees and the spring rains had turned the world to green, cleansing the air and the land. It was a perfect time to be alive, Jill decided. Jan didn't have to work and Jill had spent the morning with George and Edna, bringing them up to date on their finances.

Jill didn't do the accounting for them, they hired a CPA for that, but she had spent most of yesterday working with the accountant, and just had to go over it with Jan's neighbors this morning. They had only been home a week, but were talking about driving their motor home up into Canada since the weather was so nice. And now, Jill could relax and pour out her troubles to her older sister, in private. Grant had taken the little girls to Minneopa State Park, located just outside of town, for an afternoon of crafting, sponsored by the college.

The sisters were dressed in identical shorts and t-shirts and sunglasses. To the casual observer they were identical, although they had never considered themselves the same, and people who really knew them could easily tell them apart. They each had a soda on the table between them.

"Certifiably crazy," Jill responded.

"And you think he was interested?"

"He said he was interested in me," Jill explained again, "but when I tried to get close to him, he got very nervous."

"That he was interested was obvious last weekend when he couldn't keep his eyes off you," Jan observed. "Maybe he's not used to women making passes at him."

Jill grimaced. "That's what he said. He said I surprised

him." She looked at her sister. "Now do you really believe that a man like Dillon Hanley, a self-proclaimed bachelor, wouldn't like a woman trying to seduce him? Shoot, he would probably take full advantage of the situation. But he didn't."

"Hmm, you're right, something is going on," Jan mused. "But you told him straight out you weren't interested in marriage?"

"Exactly. And that's when he said he didn't want to have an affair. What else is there? Friendship?" She groaned. "I've been alone for six years, looking for the right man. I don't want friendship from someone who can turn my insides to cornmeal with just a look."

"I know what you mean," Jan commiserated. "After Ron made his announcement that he decided he was in love with a with someone else and up and deserted you and Penny, it tore you apart."

"And now I've come to terms with that. I understand it wasn't my fault and I really didn't have anything to do with his decision. The timing really stunk. Just having a baby, hormones all over the place." Jill shook her head. "It was a bad time, but I think I could be interested in men again," she finished. "But why couldn't I find a nice, normal man who wants a home and a family?"

"Or even just an innocent affair," Jan added. "Hmm, I don't know what to do about it either. I don't think there's anything you can do." She thought for a moment. "Maybe he's as confused as you are."

"Be serious, Jan." She laughed sarcastically. "He knows what he wants, it just isn't me. He's probably at the country club right now, making passes of his own at some luscious blonde in a bikini."

"Then let's forget about him and discuss our barbecue tomorrow night," Jan suggested. "Since George and Edna are coming, why don't you see if they want to invite that friend of theirs. What was his name? Bill Weaver?"

"And I could invite Ruth Hanley..."

"Absolutely," Jan agreed.

A little voice nagged at Jill that she was doing exactly what Dillon didn't want -- interfering in his mother's life. She shrugged it aside and turned her attention to enjoying the sun and the company.

The next evening Jill decided it was a perfect weekend. She spent her Sunday doing household chores and doing an art project with Penny. This evening was a great end to it as her friends and family gathered at Jan and Grant's home. The air was calm and the birds chirped as they headed to their nests for the night. The sinking sun, a bright red ball, could be seen to the west.

The four older adults were enjoying a game of croquet with Penny and Peggy while Jill helped Jan set the food out and Grant cooked hamburgers on the grill.

"It looks like we made a good choice," Jan observed as she and Jill stopped to laugh at the antics of Ruth, trying to play with a brace on one hand, and Bill Weaver, who had hit his ball into a bush and was now complaining good-naturedly that it was all Penny's fault. "I don't think I've ever seen Ruth as happy as she is tonight."

"It's too bad Dillon can't see her now, maybe he would understand just how lonely his mother has been since his father died. I tried to tell him, but he didn't believe me, and as good as told me to mind my own business," Jill said, before moving away from her sister to tell everyone that dinner was ready.

****

Across town, Dillon sat in the dining room of the country club with his brother. They each were drinking a beer and a had chance to talk privately.

"I just don't understand it," Jason Hanley said as he looked around at the affluent crowd gathered for a quiet, relaxing dinner after a day on the links. Meredith had gone to the ladies' room with Suzanne, leaving the brothers alone for a moment. Dillon and Jason really only had two things in common, their parents and their love of golf.

Jason had his father's dark hair, and although he was the same height as Dillon, he had a thinner build. He and his wife Meredith ran an exclusive men's shop downtown. Jason managed the retail part of the business and Meredith did the bookkeeping. Jason was a charmer, like his brother, and could probably sell used cars if he wanted to. Personally, Dillon was glad he sold men's clothing. Meredith did most of the buying and often kept Dillon in mind when she was ordering clothes. His wardrobe reflected it.

"Why would Mother prefer to go to some silly backyard picnic when she could have joined us here?" Jason complained.

"Did you ask her to come?" Dillon asked.

"I thought you were going to ask her," Jason replied with surprise. "Was I supposed to?"

Dillon didn't answer. It was true, they often forgot to ask her to join them, but if he admitted the truth, he was sure their mother would prefer a backyard barbecue. He looked around the country club. Everyone here had a partner. Ruth would have to come by herself and he was sure she wouldn't like that.

Dillon knew why he would rather be at a backyard picnic instead of here. She had gorgeous deep red hair, legs that went on and on, and she made him feel good. So good that he hadn't trusted himself to call her yesterday. Or today. He had spent almost the entire weekend at the club, playing golf with Suzanne, discussing the world of finance. And after two days of the blonde's company, Dillon could still only focus on Jill's face, could see the light in her eyes when she was laughing, when she was kissing him.

"Hello, Dillon, are you in there?" Jason was waving his hands in front of his brother's face.

"What?"

"Was I supposed to ask Mom to join us?" Jason asked. "I guess I thought she knew she's always welcome."

Dillon shook his head. "I think she likes to be asked, and actually, I did ask. She said she had other plans." He leaned across the table. "Have you ever thought of our mother as lonely?"

"Lonely? Mom? With all of her friends here?" He looked around at the people they had known all of their lives.

"Look again, Jason," Dillon advised him. "How many single, older women are there here? Or for that matter, single, older men?" He had been giving the matter some thought the last couple of days, and, much to his dismay, decided Jill made a good point.

Ruth Hanley probably would feel out of place here now, without her husband. He wasn't even sure she had been all that comfortable here when his father was alive, now that Dillon thought about it.

"What's that got to do with our dinner invitation?" Jason wanted to know. "She wouldn't be alone if she was with us."

"Who wouldn't be alone?" Meredith asked as she and Suzanne returned to the table.

"Mom," Jason answered. "Dillon's been telling me that she wouldn't have dinner with us because she's lonely."

"That's not what I said," Dillon corrected. He tried to explain to Suzanne and Meredith. "I just think she's more comfortable with friends she made on her own. And who knows, maybe she's met a man who's taking her to this backyard picnic." He wouldn't be surprised if Jill had tried a little matchmaking of her own, even after Friday night's conversation.

"A man? Our mother with a man?"

Meredith and Suzanne laughed at the disbelief on Jason's face and steered the conversation to other channels before Jason say anything else. The two women were striking contrasts. Suzanne Hall was tall with smartly styled hair that was a golden blonde, cut just below her ears and falling in kinky waves. She was athletic and smart and at ease in just about any situation. She and Dillon had been friends for as long as he could remember and were always there for each other. Everyone thought they would eventually marry, and they had talked about it, but neither could say they were in love with the other.

Meredith, on the other hand, was petite with big hazel eyes and pretty brown hair that was cut just below her shoulders. She was a perfect match for his brother, Dillon thought, kind and funny and smart as well.

Dillon sat there silently, remembering Friday night and the idiot he had made of himself. He had been over and over the scene in his house and the ride to Jill's. After he had left her and walked his mother home, Dillon had driven up to the lookout on the bluffs and sat there thinking. An idiot. That's what he finally decided he was for not taking Jill up on her offer to go to bed with him. Because that's where they were heading and they both knew it.

But now, after thinking about it almost non-stop for two days, Dillon had reached a different conclusion. He wasn't an idiot, he was in love. Maybe for the first time in his life. He had acted like an idiot, turning her down like that, but he had suddenly realized that he didn't want Jill Baxter's body without having her heart as well. He wondered if she would ever talk to him again. If she didn't, he couldn't blame her. He probably wouldn't either if he were Jill.

He was in love? Where had that come from? It couldn't be.

He looked at Suzanne, who was laughing at something Meredith said. She was a good woman, beautiful, intelligent, everything a man could ask for. Yet when he imagined her holding a baby, all he could think of was Jill holding his baby, with Penny playing nearby. His stomach tightened. Was that love?

"By God, it is!" He banged his fist on the table. Everyone in the room stopped what they were doing to stare at him.

"There's no need to get violent about it," Jason said under his breath. "If you disagree that education isn't as good as it was when we were in school, that's fine with us."

"Sorry, I don't know what came over me," Dillon apologized sheepishly, finishing his beer in one gulp. He was losing it, no doubt about it. And from the looks that the other three adults at the table exchanged, they apparently thought so as well.

"Really, I am sorry," Dillon tried again. "Why don't we go out on the patio and enjoy the evening?" he suggested, rising to assist Suzanne from her chair. The other three exchanged another knowing glance, not fooled one bit.

****

"Yoo hoo, Jill, anybody home?" Ruth Hanley called through Jill's front screen door.

"Up here, Ruth," Jill answered from her upstairs office, sighing with relief at the interruption. Penny, who usually kept her company, was watching videos on her tablet in her room. Jill had spent most of the day getting files up-to-date on several of her clients so she could meet with the accountant the next day to get some financial reports prepared.

Although she had started out as a house sitter, Jill's ability to organize had turned her into more than that. She managed several area AirBnB properties as well, and now, during the summer months, when most of the people were home, Jill still took care of hiring housekeeping and landscaping personnel, and the payment of monthly bills, leaving her older clients free to enjoy themselves and their retirement. Her business was now large enough she had to hire an accountant.

It was an arrangement that had worked out well, but it also meant keeping good records and having those available for tax purposes, one of the jobs she liked the least.

Jill had studied business before her marriage, but didn't have any set goals and had quit college to become a wife. Ron had encouraged her to stay at home and take care of him, and she had, because she loved him, which made it that much harder when he left her with a small baby and no marketable skills. Ron had offered to pay child support, but it wasn't enough for all their expenses.

If it weren't for the help of her family, she never would

have made it through those first few years. They were there when she needed them, and now she had lots of friends as well, including Ruth, the woman who had brought her son into Jill's life, even if he was threatening her sanity.

"Ruth, I am glad to see you," she greeted the other woman. "Have a seat. Or better yet, let's go back downstairs and have a cup of coffee. I think I've seen enough of this computer screen for one day."

"That's sounds wonderful, dear," Ruth said as she preceded Jill back down the steps. "I didn't mean to interrupt, I just wanted to thank you for the fun time I had last night. I can't remember when I enjoyed myself that much. George and Edna are lovely people." She sat at the table while Jill poured two cups of coffee.

"And what about Bill Weaver?" Jill inquired, sitting down across from Ruth. "Not that it's any of my business."

Jill smiled as she saw the blush spread across her friend's face.

"I guess that answers my question," she said. "I don't need to ask if you're going to see him again."

"As a matter of fact, he stopped by and ate a bite of lunch with me today," Ruth admitted. "Did you know he lives just down the street from us? He's going to help me take care of the lawn until my wrist is healed."

"But Ruth, I said I would... Oh, never mind," Jill said, as Ruth blushed again.

"Mommy, I'm hungry," Penny said, coming into the kitchen. "Hi, Grandma Ruth."

"Hello dear," Ruth greeted the little girl as she gave her a hug and a kiss.

"You're always hungry," Jill told her daughter. "Would you like a cookie and some milk?"

"One of Grandma Ruth's?" Penny asked hopefully.

The women laughed together before Jill answered. "Yes, one of Grandma Ruth's. She just made them today." Jill stood and went to the refrigerator for the milk, while Ruth got the cookies.

"Now, why don't you go sit on the front porch and eat them?" Jill suggested.

"Because you guys wanna' talk girl talk?"

"Yes, now go," her mother told her. When they were alone again, Ruth poured herself another cup of coffee, then turned the conversation to Jill.

"And what about you? Are you going to see Dillon again?"

Jill lowered her eyes and toyed with her coffee cup, unsure how to answer.

"Not that it's any of my business," Ruth added, using Jill's own words.

"You know you can stick your nose in my business anytime," Jill assured her, reaching out and patting the other woman's hand. "It's just that I don't really know. I haven't talked to him since Friday night, and you know what kind of a mood he was in then."

Ruth nodded. "I noticed. He did call me yesterday to invite me for dinner at the club last night, but I already had other plans, as you know. I've been wondering what happened to make him so growly."

It was Jill's turn to blush, but before she could answer the doorbell rang. "Saved by the bell," she muttered as she excused herself and almost ran to the door.

Not that I mind her asking, Jill thought, but what in the world do I say? I tried to seduce your son, but he wouldn't go for it. Sure, you could tell her that, Baxter. And she would laugh herself into a stroke or something. Jill breathed a sigh of relief as she opened the door. Her relief was short-lived.

"Dillon!"

"Mom, look who's here," Penny chirped from outside. "It's Dillon, the guy who took us to the circus. Can I have another cookie?"

When Jill didn't answer, the little girl shrugged her shoulders and headed for the kitchen.

"Hi Jill." He made it sound almost like a caress, his husky voice sending shivers down Jill's back. And the look he gave her encompassed her whole body, taking in the braid that curved her hair over one shoulder, the casual leggings and blouse she wore, right down to her bare feet, making her blush anew. She felt like some pioneer woman being leered at by a cowboy.

Although Dillon, in his charcoal business suit, didn't resemble any cowboy Jill had ever seen. Suave, debonair... those words only scratched the surface. He was... magnificent. The suit he wore to perfection only gave a hint of the man wearing it. But Jill remembered in detail the muscles and hard planes of his chest, the way his hair felt beneath her fingers, all springy... She didn't realize she was staring until he cleared his throat, a habit she was coming to love. He only did it when he was uncomfortable and there was some satisfaction that she could make him uncomfortable.

"Um, have you seen my mother? Her car is home, but she isn't."

"Oh, sure, she's in the kitchen," Jill said, recovering.

Had it only been three days since they parted at that very door? "Come in. Ruth," she called, "there's someone here to see you."

"Dillon! What are you doing here? This is Monday, isn't

it?" His mother came bustling from the kitchen.

Dillon and Jill shared a smile. If Jill hadn't known better, she would have guessed the scene Friday night had never taken place. It was almost uncanny how they seemed to know what the other was thinking, except, Jill thought, when it came to feelings about the other.

"Yes Mother, it's Monday. I just came by to see if you want me to mow your lawn one evening this week." Never mind that he had never offered before. She had a broken wrist now and needed more help. He wouldn't mention that he needed an excuse for dropping by.

It was the women's turn to share a smile. Neither was sure why Dillon had come by, but they both knew it wasn't to mow lawns.

"No, I don't think so," Ruth said. "A nice gentleman from down the block has offered to do it for me."

"Oh?" Dillon's eyebrows rose as he looked suspiciously at Jill.

She shrugged innocently and turned back to Ruth. Jill had done her part in matchmaking for her friend, and it had turned out well. She wasn't about to tell Dillon all about it so he could spoil it.

"Anyway, I suppose I should be getting home," Ruth was continuing. "Thanks for the coffee, Jill." She turned to leave, then noticed that Dillon hadn't moved. "Dillon dear, are you coming?"

"What? Oh, sure, in just a minute. I'd like to talk to Jill."

"All right then, but then I insist you stay for supper," Ruth said. "I just don't get to see my boys enough," she muttered as she went out the front door.

Dillon shook his head as his mother left, then turned

to Jill.

"I can't believe she just said that, considering we had a family dinner without her last night, because she was at Jan and Grant's," he said, still shaking his head. "Did she have a good time?"

"She said she did," Jill said, "but maybe you should ask her. How was your evening?"

Terrible, he wanted to say. The evening, the whole weekend had been terrible. No, that wasn't quite true. The time he had spent with Jill on Friday night had been very special, right up until he had almost literally kicked her out of his home. And last night had been a startling revelation. A wonderful revelation. After he left the club and took Suzanne home, he had gone home and swam laps in the pool, thinking things over, wanting to make sure he was correct in assessing his feelings. This was too big a step to take without being sure.

Suzanne had been very understanding when he told her that he wouldn't be spending so much time with her.

"You went and fell in love on me, didn't you?" Suzanne had asked softly when he left her at her door. He couldn't deny it, he wouldn't deny it. So he explained about Jill, without mentioning her name, how she had snuck up on him and stole his heart.

"Hit you right over the head." Suzanne nodded. She had taken his hand in hers as she continued. "We knew a long time ago we weren't in love with each other, so it was just a matter of time until one of us found someone else. It's all right, really, but do you suppose we could still be friends? I know that's asking a lot, but your friendship means so much to me."

Dillon was unsure of what to say, but Suzanne was

right. They had been friends for a long time, and no matter who he was in love with, that friendship was important. He also realized that he probably knew more about Suzanne than anyone in the world, and that was important to him. And so they parted, a little sadly, but knowing that to grow they must move on to other relationships.

"Um, hello? You said you had something to talk to me about," Jill reminded him.

"I did?" he asked, trying to recall what they had been saying. Oh, yes. He stepped closer. Jill backed up.

"Nervous?"

Jill licked her lips. "Why would I be nervous?"

"No reason that I know of," he said, stepping closer again.

"You said you wanted to talk to me..."

"I lied. What I really want to do is kiss you." He took another step before Jill could react and stood with his hands in his pockets. He lowered his lips to hers to make contact, leaving their bodies apart.

He tasted as good as ever, Jill thought. Better. Wonderful, she decided as she let her hands go where they wanted and wrapped them around his neck. She felt the touch of Dillon's hands as he wrapped them around her waist, drawing her up against his hardness. She wondered hazily how she had ever lived without this man's kisses, which could send her senses reeling in a matter of minutes. Or seconds, Jill wasn't sure how long it lasted. Nor did she care, all she knew was that she wanted it to go on forever.

She moaned in protest when Dillon finally ended the kiss and opening her eyes, looked into his eyes, filled with desire and probably reflecting her own.

"Hello."

"Hello," Jill returned as Penny came back into the living room.

"What'cha doin' guys?"

"Nothing," Jill said guiltily, backing away from Dillon.

"I was kissing your mother," Dillon told the little girl, ignoring the glaring look he got from Jill.

"Why?"

This time Jill folded her arms and smiled.

"Because I wanted to," Dillon answered calmly. Penny considered this for a moment, then shrugged, apparently satisfied with the answer. "I put my glass on the counter and I washed my hands. Can I go outside and play now?"

"Yes, of course, but stay in the yard," Jill told her as she raced out the door.

"Do you tell her that every time she goes outside?" Dillon asked, smiling. He looked oddly content, sitting on the arm of the sofa, relaxed, with his legs stretched out in front of him and his arms crossed on his chest. He looked like a man who knew exactly what he wanted out of life. He certainly didn't look confused to Jill.

Jill nodded, silently wondering about the change in him.

"Just about. I don't think you can tell a child that age too many times to do things that will keep her safe, like watching for cars and not talking to strangers."

"It's been hard for you, hasn't it, raising a child alone?" he mused, coming to stand near her again, caressing her arms.

"There have been times when I wished she wasn't my sole responsibility," Jill admitted, "because what happens if I make a mistake? There's no one to blame but me. On the other hand, every time she accomplishes something new, I get to take all the credit."

"And you should be proud of her, she's a very special little girl," Dillon said.

"Thanks, but I'm sure you didn't come all the way over here just to talk about Penny." His hands on her arms were driving her senses crazy, sending her heart racing again.

"That's true, but I didn't really think you wanted her to see us doing this again," he said as his lips claimed hers again.

Jill almost wished he would quit kissing her since every time he did, she found it impossible to think. On the other hand, she never wanted it to end, except to lead to other things, more intimate touches. She wanted his touch on her bare skin, to have them become one. She wanted to make love to this man, right now, right on the living room floor, if necessary, any place as long as it could stop the sweet ache she felt in her stomach as the kiss deepened, drawing deep into her soul, possessing her. Once again, she felt Dillon's desire as their bodies molded into one, her softness into his hardness. And he wanted her, Jill knew.

But she was confused. "I thought you didn't want to have an affair," she blurted out as she finally got her emotions under control and twisted out of his embrace, trying to calm her breathing.

"I don't."

"Then want do you want?" Jill almost wailed. Dillon Hanley had to be one of the most frustrating men she had ever met. She felt like she was on a roller coaster ride. First he said he didn't want to get involved, or married, to be exact, then he kissed her. Later he said he didn't want to get involved, then he kissed her. Then, when Jill kissed him, he said he didn't want to have an affair, and now he was kissing her again, but he still didn't want to have an affair. He was definitely trying to drive her crazy. As loony as a goony bird.

"I want to marry you."

Chapter 6

Jill stood still and stared at him. She knew her mouth was open, she just couldn't seem to make her muscles work to close it.

"Are you crazy?" she finally shouted at him. "You aren't thinking clearly. We don't even know each other. We've only had one date. And three days ago you practically ran away at the mention of the word 'marriage.' Again, are you crazy?"

"I don't think so," he answered calmly and confidently, sitting back down on the arm of the sofa while Jill paced.

"Then I must be," she muttered. She stopped in front of him. "You did say marry, didn't you?"

He nodded, and Jill banged her hand against her temple before she started pacing again.

"You mean, you came over here today just to tell me you want to marry me?"

He nodded again, enjoying her disbelief. He still couldn't completely believe it himself, but the more he thought about it, the more he was sure he had made the right decision.

"And you honestly think that just because all of a sudden you decide you want to get married," she raised her voice, making it sound squeaky and gesturing wildly with her hands, "I'll just say yes?"

This time Dillon smiled as he nodded.

"That confirms it, you're crazy." And me too. There, I've finally gone off the edge, Jill thought inanely. "Get out," she pointed to the door. When he didn't move, she went over to the door and yanked it open. "I mean it, out. Go have supper with your mother, go back to the country club and your blondes, anything, just get out!"

"Jill, honey..." How did she know about the blondes? Never mind, Hanley, you may have a problem here, he thought.

"Don't you 'honey' me, you, you....I don't even have a word!"

Definitely a problem, Dillon decided.

Jill was starting to shake. "You told me you didn't want marriage, and I could live with that, then you said you didn't want an affair. Well, now I don't want marriage, and as far as I'm concerned you can say goodbye to an affair too. In fact," she shouted, "you can just say goodbye."

Dillon decided that since things weren't going quite the way he had planned, maybe he should retreat for the moment. She obviously didn't want anything to do with his new plan.

"Okay, I'll leave," he said, "but when I come back, and I will be back, we're going to sit down and talk about this rationally." He sauntered confidently out the door, stopping to give Jill a quick kiss on the cheek as he went.

The door rattled the windows on either side as Jill slammed it shut.

"Damn the man," she muttered, sinking down on the sofa. "Who does he think he is?"

No doubt about it, he was out to drive her crazy, Jill decided. Marriage. To Dillon Hanley. She had tried not to even let herself even consider the idea, appealing though it might be. And she wasn't going to think about it now, either. She jumped up and went to the kitchen, pulling out pots and pans to start making dinner for her and Penny.

Why had he changed his mind? Why did he want marriage all of a sudden? Cook, Baxter, don't think, she admonished herself. It didn't work though as her brain refused to listen. It just didn't add up. They had only known each other a week, and while that might be time to get to know each other well enough to sleep together, it wasn't long enough to know if they were compatible enough to live together forever. And last week he was adamant about not getting married.

There was no way he could have changed his mind so drastically, when they hadn't even seen each other, to the point that he wanted to spend the rest of his life with her. Was there? No, definitely not. She pulled out the ingredients for macaroni and cheese, one of Penny's favorite dishes, put water in the pan and turned on the burner. Jill had made the dish so many times that there was little chance that she would mess it up, even as distracted as she was. She was distracted, that was for sure.

Maybe he was confused, just as Jan said. But he didn't look or act confused and if he wasn't, then what was he up to? Her mind battled the question the whole time she was fixing the meal and throughout it. She paid very little attention to Penny's chattering, trying to come to grips with the question before Dillon came back. He would, she was sure, probably after his own meal with Ruth. And then what would she say?

Maybe she should go visit Jan. No, that wouldn't solve anything. It would be running away. But her head would be clearer if she talked it out. Oh, what was she going to do? Jill asked herself as she cleared the table and washed the dishes. Penny had gone to watch television in the living room, and for once, Jill was too distracted to tell her to turn the volume down to a reasonable level.

Twenty minutes later, Jill wasn't any less confused but she was determined. There wasn't going to be a marriage, there wasn't going to be an affair. She was done with all of it and was going back to the safe routine of her life.

When the doorbell rang, signaling Dillon's return, she knew she had to talk to him. Not that she could have avoided him if she wanted to except by slipping out the back door, because Penny had already let him in.

"Mom, Dillon is back," Penny announced from the living room.

"Mom's in the kitchen," she directed Dillon rather than leave her program.

Jill barely had time to slip on her sandals, lying forgotten all afternoon under the kitchen table, before Dillon walked confidently through the door. She decided she might need the extra confidence the shoes gave her.

"You're not going to throw me out again, are you?" he asked by way of greeting, carefully watching her reaction.

"I'm tempted," she returned, "but I've decided I want an explanation first." Or he could just stand there so she could look at him. He had shed his tie, vest and suit jacket and un-buttoned his shirt at the neck and his tanned arms extended from his rolled-up sleeves. He looked good enough to eat.

"For what?" He hoped it wasn't about the blondes.

"Don't play games with me, Hanley," she warned. Keep your mind on the conversation, Jill told herself. "Why do you want to marry me?"

"Ah, well..." He cleared his throat. He hadn't intended to blurt it out earlier, he thought that he would just date her and things would fall into place. But she was so direct. It was one of the things he loved about her, but it had made him say something she wasn't prepared to deal with. He could just tell her the truth, that he loved her. And would she believe him? Probably not, after Friday's performance. Maybe he should go for part of the truth.

"Jill, I'm thirty-two years old and I think it's time I settled down," he started. "We get along well and Penny likes me..."

"Dillon Hanley, that is such a bunch of bull," Jill said. He was thirty-two. She hadn't even known that. But then there were many things she didn't know about this man. Never mind, she was straying from the point. "You were thirty-two last week and then you were worried about your reputation as a bachelor. Now, all of a sudden, it's time to settle down?"

Damn, she was just too shrewd. He tried again.

"What's wrong with that? I changed my mind, all right?"

"And Friday night? Are you going to tell me what that was all about?"

Not if I can help it, he thought. "Look Jill, I know I messed up Friday night. Can't we just forget that?"

Jill considered it for a moment, then walked straight to him so they stood nose to nose. She curved her arms seductively around his neck.

"Does that mean we can make love?" she breathed in his ear.

"Oh, Jill, that sounds so good," he couldn't stop himself from saying. "Um, right now?" Sparks of desire ignited in the pit of his stomach, making his body tighten in response. He couldn't think when she did that, but he knew there was a reason he shouldn't take her right there in the kitchen, on the table, or the floor, it didn't matter. All coherent thought fled as his arms crept around her waist as he kissed her, only aware of his need for this woman.

Jill felt as if she would burst with sexual release when his lips finally made contact with her own. That must be a "yes," and oh, she was glad. No, no, no, she didn't want this. She wanted her life back.

Her body apparently felt otherwise as it responded. Whatever else Jill didn't know about Dillon Hanley, she knew the feel of his aroused body, pressed into her. And she knew that she wanted him, that she loved him. Loved him? Don't think about that, she told herself, it should be enough to desire him. And it was, right at that moment, as his hands followed a path down her back to her butt, and then pulled her to him so that his hardness pressed against her pelvis.

"Dillon, I want you," she murmured when his lips left hers to travel down to her neckline. Jill threw her head back to allow him access. His hands found their way under her full skirt to travel back up her bare thighs to where her panties blocked their way, waves of passion rushed over her.

"Hey Mom, I'm hungry."

Dillon and Jill bolted at the sound of the voice from the other room. Dillon took several steadying breaths. That was the reason they couldn't make love here, now.

Jill straightened her skirt, shocked that she could have forgotten her surroundings like that, and forgotten that Penny was in the next room. A moment later Penny came through the door.

"I'm hungry."

"Me too," Dillon muttered, sitting down at the table and trying once again to control his desire. Actually, it was amazing that after an interruption at that point that he wasn't lying on the floor, writhing in pain. He smiled at the thought and met Jill's gaze.

How could he laugh at a time like this? Jill wondered. She felt like she had been within inches of Heaven's door, only to have it slammed in her face. And there Dillon was, sitting calmly, acting like nothing had happened. Not that anything had happened, except that Jill's world had turned upside down. And next time it happened, she wasn't stopping until it righted itself of its own accord. Not trusting herself to speak to Dillon, Jill addressed Penny.

"How can you be hungry? We just ate an hour ago."

Penny shrugged. "Can I have a cookie?"

"You can have an apple," her mother told her. "You had cookies this afternoon."

"All right, I'll have an apple," Penny said, going to the refrigerator. She could tell by her mother's tone of voice that an apple was the best she was going to do. She raced back to the living room after she got the fruit, leaving the two adults alone again.

"Well."

"Well."

They spoke at the same time. Jill sat down at the table and rested her chin on her hands.

"What now?" she asked.

Dillon ran his fingers through his hair, messing it more than what Jill had earlier, in a gesture Jill was beginning to become familiar with and love.

"I don't know," he said, leaning back in his chair, "but there's no way we can have 'an affair' as you call it, with her around. I'm just not up to it." He paused. "I do know that we should stay at least five feet apart unless we want to continue where we left off."

"Well, that sounds promising," Jill mused, "but you know I can't just dump Penny every time my hormones go wild."

Dillon thought for a moment. "We could send her over to Mom's," he suggested.

"That's fine. Do you want to explain why to them? I didn't think so," she added as Dillon shook his head.

"Camp?" he tried hopefully.

Jill shook her head. "She doesn't go to sumer camp," she said. "She's not old enough."

"The French Foreign Legion?"

She shook her head again.

"I didn't think so. I can't even believe we're having this conversation," Dillon said. "It isn't very romantic."

"And what do you know about romance?" Jill asked. "Forget I said that," she added as Dillon's brows rose. "I forgot I was talking to a professional playboy."

"Well, I wouldn't say professional," he teased. "But I'm right, admit it."

"Okay, I admit it," she laughed. "The question is, what are we going to do about it?" She didn't mention the decision she had made only minutes before to end this whole thing.

He stood and came around the table, pulling Jill from her chair. "Oh no, you don't, Hanley," she said, backing away. "We're not alone, and that means five feet."

He looked hurt. "All I was going to suggest was that we take things slow. Get to know each other. Date." Dillon said the word like it was distasteful.

"Exclusively?"

"Definitely." He wasn't any good to anyone else anyway, with Jill always on his mind.

"Want to shake on it?" Jill offered her hand.

"Seal it with a kiss?" he murmured, leaning toward her and pulling back her hand.

Jill jerked her hand out of his. "Oh no you don't, Hanley! Five feet!"

****

Dillon kept his word, and his kisses to himself the rest of the week, but he came by each evening, either for dinner or shortly after. They worked in Jill's garden one evening, took a walk with Penny to the neighborhood park and shared ice cream cones another evening. They sat on Ruth's porch with the older woman Thursday evening, watching Penny chase fireflies.

It was all very nice, Jill thought, if not very romantic. Of course, the friendly goodnight kisses she received each night on her front porch were tantalizing, but not enough. And they didn't stay five feet away from each other all of the time, but their touches, usually in the presence of Penny, were casual. It was if they were testing their willpower. Well, Jill had already decided that her willpower wasn't enough to combat the hold the man had on her.

Jan told Jill she really had gone over the edge if she could actually keep her hands off Dillon. "I know I wouldn't be able to keep my hands off Grant," she said.

"I remember," Jill said, laughing. "I was so glad when you two got married, and could give the rest of us some relief. But I've learned my lesson," she continued. "I hope. Dillon wants to take it slower, and I've been trying. I'm just waiting for him to realize that slower is not always necessarily better."

Jan's eyebrows rose. "So why not just marry him?" Jill had already told her sister about Monday's conversation with Dillon. "That's what he wants."

Jill thought about the question as she toyed with her salad. The two had gotten together for lunch at a restaurant near Jan's office as was their custom on Fridays. It gave them a chance to talk over the week and make any plans necessary for the next couple of days, since they usually did at least one activity together on the weekend.

"I'm not convinced that is what he wants, and I don't think either one of us is ready for marriage, Jan. I think you were right, and he's confused," she said. "I want him to be sure. I actually made the decision to end this whole thing and go back to my old life. I just don't need the drama. But that clearly didn't work. One kiss and I was mush."

"So what are you going to do about it?' Jan asked.

"I've come up with a plan," Jill said.

"A plan," Jan repeated. "What is this great plan?" She tried not to smile. Jill was on the end of a losing battle. She just didn't know it yet.

"I'm going to seduce him," she announced. "I just need your help."

Jan raised her eyebrows. "My help?" she asked. "How could I possibly help?"

"I just need a new dress and you to keep Penny tonight," she replied. "We're going to a play downtown, so after... well, we'll see what happens."

"This is a bad idea, Jill," Jan said. "Don't you think getting him into bed is a little dishonest?"

"Maybe," Jill conceded, her conscience getting the best of her. "But I think if we went to bed, he might realize that he has been getting his honor confused with his heart."

"And his body," Jan finished for her. "You love him though, don't you?"

****

The trouble with sisters who think the same things you do, Jill thought as she was getting ready to go out with Dillon, is that sometimes they know what you are thinking before you do. Love. And Dillon Hanley? In less than two weeks? Jill shook her head at the thought, but wasn't sure she could deny it. Her body had known but she had been so busy telling herself that marriage wasn't what Dillon wanted, that she hadn't realized her true feelings for him until Jan had verbalized them for her.

Jill was in shock for the remainder of lunch, responding

to Jan's conversation automatically. They had made plans for Penny to spend the night at Jan's, since Jill and Dillon were going to the theater and Ruth had made other plans for the evening.

At least that was one romance that was looking good, Jill thought wryly. Ruth and Bill Weaver had hit it off well and were going out tonight as well. And now it was time for Jill to start working on her own romance. Step one was sending Penny to Jan's house. Despite what she had told Dillon on Monday about dumping the little girl, there were times when adults needed to be alone. Jill knew better than anyone that Penny didn't care for theater unless it starred Big Bird.

The dress she and Jan had picked out after lunch for her to wear was the second step. A cream-colored satin overlaid with cream-colored lace, the fitted top dropped to her hips before gently flaring and caressing the tops of her calves. With a scooped neck and lace sleeves, all Jill needed to accent it were pearls in her ears and around her neck. She brushed her hair off her forehead until it laid in graceful waves around her shoulders. A pair of matching shoes and she was ready.

And the third step... well, she would get to that later.

Right now the door bell was ringing, signaling Dillon's arrival.

"Come in, come in," Jill welcomed Dillon cheerfully a few seconds later.

"Said the spider to the fly," Dillon muttered, entering. Why did this woman make him nervous? So far all she had done was open the door and smile at him. He hadn't been prepared for that dress though. It wasn't the first time he had seen her dressed up, but she looked so elegant, so regal. He wondered briefly if he could skip the play and just spend the evening discovering the woman beneath the alluring lace.

"What was that?" she asked, picking up a shawl and her clutch that held her phone. Going out with Dillon Hanley was worth it just to see what he would wear. Tonight he was wearing a linen sports coat with crisp linen slacks and brown shoes. He must have a bigger closet than she did, Jill thought idly. Between the two of them tonight, the only color either one sported was Jill's hair and Dillon's striped tie.

"Nothing," Dillon was answering. "Say, where's Penny?" He looked around the room. "Over at Mom's?"

"No, she's spending the night at Jan's. Ruth had other plans for this evening," Jill said, turning on the porch light and turning off the inside lamp. She motioned for Dillon to precede her out the door so she could lock it after they were out.

"Mom didn't say she was going out," Dillon mused as he ushered Jill to the car. He didn't want to think about the fact that Penny wouldn't be home all night, he wanted to make it through the evening without ravishing Jill. "And Jason didn't say anything about her going over there."

"I don't think she's going over to Jason's," Jill admitted, getting in. "She said something about a movie."

"By herself?" he asked as they backed out of her driveway.

"Well, no, I don't think so."

"You set her up, didn't you?"

"Um...well..."

"You did. I can't believe it," he said. "With that man you were talking about?"

Jill nodded. "Bill Weaver. But Dillon, really, all I did was introduce them. It's not like this is a blind date I set up. They decided they enjoyed each other's company and took it from there. Besides, if he keeps her busy, she can't be matchmaking for you."

"I think she's already done her part with that," Dillon said, grimacing. "She probably knew that once I saw you I wouldn't be able to resist you and that's why she agreed so easily to let me finish painting her house."

"Thank you, I think," she said, reaching out and gently placing her hand on his shoulder. "But enough about her, what play are we going to see tonight?"

"It's a comedy, and features a guest artist in the title role," he explained as he parked the car near the downtown performing arts center. They would have a short walk, but neither minded since the evening was nice. They agreed it had been a nice spring so far, and their conversation drifted to the farmers that Dillon worked with on loans and how they were faring.

Dillon wasn't surprised that Jill could converse on such a subject, anyone who was resourceful enough to start providing a much-needed service for the area's older citizens was likely well-versed in other subjects. And she had told him she studied business in college but never graduated, Dillon remembered as the curtain rose on the play. He wondered why she had never gone back and gotten her degree. He made a silent note to ask her about it as the play started and claimed their attention.

Jill's concentration was more on the man sitting close to her than the play, even though it was superbly presented. The Merely Players theater group was well known in southern Minnesota and their performances were almost always sold out. But the brush of Dillon's sleeve on Jill's bare arm, the way their legs touched, claimed a good part of her attention.

She was almost glad when the house lights came on, signaling the end of the play.

"It was wonderful, wasn't it?" Dillon asked as she gathered her belongings.

"What? Oh yes, I really enjoyed it," Jill answered, hoping Dillon was talking about the play. Of course, just being close to him was wonderful, even if it was torture. And since she had discovered she was in love with him, it was even more wonderful, because now she had a plan.

The sun had long set as they wandered out of the building, and set off for the car. "Would you like to stop somewhere for a drink?" Dillon asked her.

"I don't think so," Jill said, appearing to consider the question, although she knew exactly what she wanted. It was time for step three. "Too noisy."

"A drive?"

"Too dark."

He looked at her in exasperation. "Are you ready to go home already?" Jill just shook her head as they reached the car.

"That only leaves my place, and we'll be alone there," he said, unlocking the doors. "And you know what happens when we're alone."

Jill didn't answer until they were on their way. "I like what happens when we're alone, don't you?"

Dillon groaned and drove a little faster as she put her hand on that sensitive part of his thigh, sending ripples of pleasure through his body.

"Is this going to be a repeat of last week?" he asked.

"Only if you turn me down," Jill said, "and I thought we agreed to forget about last week."

How could he forget, Dillon wondered? The way she had smelled, the way her breasts had been crushed against his chest, the way she had tasted. No, he couldn't forget as his body tightened in that now familiar way he associated with Jill.

"Are you sure?" he asked, turning to face her as he pulled into his driveway and turned off the motor.

Jill nodded. "Maybe I should be the one asking you that. Are you sure?"

"If I was any more sure, we would never make it to the front door," he murmured, touching her cheek with his knuckles and caressing gently. "You know, though, I don't want an affair. I want it all."

Jill didn't hear him as his touch sent shivers of desire through her body. Their eyes met for a long moment and they were unaware of anything but each other, then almost as one their lips moved toward each other and touched, tasted and reacquainted themselves with the other. Only when Dillon became aware of the steering wheel stuck in his ribs did he break the kiss.

"Ouch," he said, rubbing his side. "That probably wasn't a good idea."

"Oh, I don't know, the idea was fine, it was the location we missed on," Jill teased him as she opened her door and got out. She waited on the drive until Dillon came around to escort her.

This time when she entered his home, Jill was familiar with its layout, and laying her purse and phone on a low table, wandered to the patio door that opened into the courtyard with its inviting pool. She wondered what it would be like, making love with Dillon in the tempting pool of water.

Dillon followed her, having turned on only one lamp. He removed his jacket and tie, and came to stand behind her, putting his arms around her waist and resting his chin on her shoulder, inhaling the clean, fresh scent of her hair.

"This is nice. Penny would love having a pool in the backyard," Jill said softly.

"Maybe she can come over some time and swim," Dillon

said, moving her hair from her neck so his could plant small kisses there. "It's heated."

Even better for making love. "I guess that's how you stay in such good shape."

"You think I have a good shape?" he whispered against her throat.

"Um hmm. For a banker."

"I suppose you think I should be short and bald, with a pot belly," he chuckled huskily.

"That's what my banker looks like," Jill said, turning in his arms. His lips on the sensitive skin of her throat were creating havoc with her senses, making her want more.

"Maybe you should get a new banker," Dillon said, claiming her lips.

"I'm working on it," she murmured a long moment later. "What kind of interest can you give me?"

"I'll show you interest," he growled, scooping her into his arms and carrying her up the stairs to his bedroom.

Neither noticed as one of Jill's shoes bounced down the steps and the other fell onto the floor near the bedroom door. He set her down only long enough to turn on a bedside lamp, casting a warm glow on the room and giving Jill an impression of roominess.

Then his lips were on hers again, his body pressing into hers. Suddenly the layers of clothing were too much of a barrier for Jill. She began unbuttoning his shirt, eager to reacquaint herself with Dillon's body.

He, in turn, brought one hand from its resting place on her hip to her zipper, drawing it slowly down. The dress slipped off of Jill's shoulders and Dillon trailed kisses across her collarbone. Jill moved slightly and the dress fell into a pool of lace at her feet, leaving her clad only in a white lacy bra and matching panties.

"Oh, Jill, you're beautiful," Dillon whispered as he stepped back from her. He had dreamed of this moment ever since he had met her.

"You're not so bad yourself," Jill murmured, drawing him close once again and running her hands around his waist, untucking his shirt as she went, feeling the strength of the muscles of his back as they rippled in response to her touch.

It was only moments before Dillon had his clothes off and was lowering Jill to his bed. The sheet was cool on her back, Jill thought inanely. She could feel the hardness of his arousal against her hip bone and her stomach tightened. He kissed one strap of her bra off of her shoulder, then the other, moving his hands to her breasts.

Jill's breath caught in her throat at the intimate touch, then gasped out loud as his lips caught one tightened bud and pulled gently before his mouth closed over it.

He gave the same treatment to Jill's other breast, making her breathing ragged. She felt the curl of passion start deep down in her belly and radiate in waves. It had been so long since a man had treated her with such reverence. Even Ron had not been able to provoke these feelings. And when Dillon's lips traveled tantalizingly slow down her stomach, Jill felt every muscle react in pleasure. A moment later her underclothes were joining their other clothes on the floor and her body was open to Dillon's intimate perusal.

"Perfection," he murmured into her abdomen as he kissed her there. His fingers had found the center of her arousal and were creating chaos within her body. Her body arched instinctively toward the source of its pleasure.

"Dillon," she breathed, tugging at his hair. She had been caressing the silky strands, loving the feel, but now she was impatient. "Come to me, now, please."

Dillon groaned as he moved up her body. He wanted so much to give this woman pleasure, but her plea was more than his body, which he had already pushed to his limit of control, could take.

"Are you sure?" he wanted to know, before he let his body take over his mind.

Jill nodded, trailing her fingers down the hard planes of his stomach to his throbbing hardness. "I've never been this sure about anything," she said softly, using her other hand to draw his lips to hers. I love you, her heart was beating, but she knew she couldn't say the words.

Dillon's body jerked in reaction to her movements and he knew he couldn't have stopped then if the building was crashing down around them. After a short pause, he moved back over her and into her warmth, making them both sigh with relief as Jill opened to receive all of him And then they moved together, became one, aware only of the intimate dance of their bodies as they pleasured each other, their hearts drumming out the beat. The age-old dance between man and woman moved faster and faster, until they were dizzy with the sensations of lips on lips, skin on dampened skin, breath mingling as they strove for passionate release. And when they thought they could no longer stand the pleasure, the dance caught them up. Breathing stopped. Time stopped. Only the feeling continued. And the beating of their hearts.

It was some time before either spoke, or was able to. They rested comfortably in the position their lovemaking had created, until Dillon became concerned about his weight on his lovely Jill.

"Don't move," she pleaded, trying to keep him in place.

He chuckled softly. "I'm heavy, and I'm not moving very

far, I promise." Dillon left their legs entwined and snuggled his head on her shoulder, breathing in her scent, loving the feel of her, loving her, although he dared not say the words. He rested a hand on her stomach, drawing small circles there with his fingers, igniting Jill's passion once again.

"Dillon?"

"Hmm?"

"Thanks back there, for protecting us." She was touched that he thought of that, somewhere in her plans it had been forgotten. And although she loved him and would love some day to have his baby, a tiny little sister or brother for Penny, it was important that they didn't rush into it. A baby was not a good reason to get married.

"You're welcome." He was surprised that she mentioned it without making any cracks about being prepared, but then she was continually surprising him with her sensitivity. He also knew that he couldn't live with himself if he trapped her into a marriage she wasn't ready for by getting her pregnant.

And Dillon still wanted marriage, he was sure of his love now if he wasn't before. Now he just had to convince Jill.

"Do you have any idea what you're doing to me?"

His hand stilled for a moment, and then she could feel him smile against her shoulder. His fingers started their sweet torture again.

Afterward Dillon turned the lamp off and they slept for a time, sated for the moment, content to hold one another.

The sky was tinged with pink when the feel of Dillon's lips on her breast woke Jill. "It's time to go home," he whispered.

"Home," Jill repeated groggily. "Oh! Penny..." She sat straight up.

He knew what she was thinking and knew her concern was real, but he couldn't keep his eyes off of her perfectly-shaped breasts that had been revealed as the blanket fell to Jill's waist when she sat up. "Relax, she's at Jan's," he said, suddenly distracted.

Jill followed his gaze and suddenly felt shy. She pulled the blanket up to cover herself. Dillon pulled it back down and bent his head to savor the taste of her one more time. As a result, it was some time before the two ventured out into the dawn.

"Where to?" Dillon asked her as he backed out of the drive. He had taken a quick shower and dressed in jeans and a sweatshirt, making Jill feel out of place in her lace dress from the night before.

Jill looked at the clock on the car's dashboard. "It's too early to get Penny from Jan's. Why don't we go to my house? I'll fix us some breakfast." She certainly didn't want to go anywhere else, dressed as she was.

"Sounds good." He headed the car in the direction of Jill's home.

Neither talked much as they drove, wanting to keep the mood of the past few hours for as long as they could, not wanting to analyze their reactions to one another.

Once they arrived at Jill's, she showered and changed into jeans and a sweatshirt, feeling much more comfortable. When she came back in the kitchen Dillon was busy fixing pancakes and bacon. They were ravished, and when they sat down to eat, the only noise in the kitchen was the clink of their silverware.

Jill was on her third pancake and Dillon his fifth when a knock sounded at the back door. They looked at each other in surprise, before Jill shrugged her shoulders and rose to answer it.

"Ruth!" Jill exclaimed as she opened the door.

Dillon turned around in his chair. "Mother?"

Chapter 7

Ruth rushed in with Bill on her heels.

"We were beginning to wonder if you two were ever coming back," she said, looking from one to the other.

"Mom, what's wrong?" Dillon asked, rising. He took in the older couple's disheveled appearance. "Where have you been? Are you all right?"

"Now, now, there's nothing wrong," Ruth assured her son. "I just forgot my key and Jill has the spare. We waited for hours for you to bring her home, but then gave up."

"And you spent the night with this man?" Dillon nearly shouted. "Why didn't you just call?"

The older couple looked at one another. Bill was a retired mailman and had lost his wife to cancer four years earlier. His gray hair was clipped short to his head, only as long as his neatly trimmed and equally gray mustache and beard. He had lost some of the fitness he had during his time in the Marines and preferred jeans and an old shirt to the slacks and nice shirt he was wearing now. He loved to talk and he laughed easily but he wasn't smiling now. He stood with Ruth as she answered her son.

"I tried to call," Ruth replied after clearing her throat. "Both of you. Neither of you answered your phone."

Dillon and Jill looked at each other, then pulled out their phones. Both had several missed calls from Ruth at different times during the night. They looked at each other again and Dillon opened his mouth to say something. Jill decided it was a good time to step in.

"Would you two like some coffee? Or breakfast?" she asked, pulling out chairs for Bill and Ruth. "We were just having pancakes."

"A cup of coffee would be wonderful," Ruth said, and Bill nodded. "But don't bother with breakfast, we found an all-night café open near Faribault. . . "

"Faribault? What were you doing there?" Dillon exploded. He glared at Bill.

"Eating breakfast. I just told you," Ruth said calmly.

"Hey, look," Bill inserted as he accepted a cup of coffee from Jill, "it's not like we spent the night at my house. We just came over to get Ruth's key. There's no reason to get bent out of shape."

"He's right, Dillon," Jill added, hoping to calm the situation. She should have predicted Dillon might react this way to the news that Bill and Ruth spent the night together, but then, she had no way of knowing that was what they would do. Jill admitted to herself that even she was a little surprised, but considering their own behavior, she and Dillon were in no position to judge anyone. "I'll go get your key, Ruth."

Dillon sat back down at the table and turned to his mother. "And what did you do all night, before you drove to Faribault?"

Ruth and Bill exchanged looks that made Dillon uneasy, before Ruth spoke.

"Well, we went to a movie..."

"You know," Bill interrupted, "they just don't make movies like they used to. Whatever happened to the movies like we watched when we were young?"

Ruth nodded in understanding. "I really miss soft, romantic movies. Today, it's all rock music or space creatures. And so much violence."

Dillon looked from one to the other. What was going on here? They were talking like they had forgotten he was even in the room. He cleared his throat.

"Then what?"

"What? Oh, well, you know. Probably the same thing you two did," Ruth said.

"What?" Dillon shouted, jumping out of his chair, startling both of them. He grabbed Bill by the shirtfront and almost yanked him out of his chair. "You did what with my mother?!"

"Talked," Ruth said, rising and rushing to Bill's side. "We talked for hours and hours. And put him down. You almost gave both of us a heart attack," she complained as Dillon let loose and Bill sank back down, relieved.

"Isn't that what you two did?" Ruth asked as Jill came back in the room. "Or need I ask?" She noted Dillon's guilty look.

"What did we do?" Jill asked, handing Ruth her key.

"Talk. That's what we did also, right Jill?" Dillon growled.

"Oh, right. Sure," she answered, turning back to Ruth and Bill. "Has he been grilling you?"

"Yes, he has," Bill said, "and I can't say I liked it one bit. Come on Ruth, I'll walk you home."

"Ruth, I'll talk to you later," Jill promised, opening the door as Bill and Ruth rose to leave.

"I think he's been around Penny too long," she whispered to the older lady as she went out of the door. Jill watched them walk down the driveway before she turned back to Dillon, who was sitting and glaring into his cup.

He looked up as Jill closed the door and started clearing away dishes, wondering what she should say to him. He had treated both Ruth and Bill appallingly.

"This is all your fault, you know," Dillon stated.

"These dishes? If I remember right, you helped too," she said tightly, loading the dishwasher.

He shook his head as he rose to help her. "You've taken my mother and corrupted her. Dammit, Jill," he said, dropping the silverware he was carrying and taking her by the shoulders, "she spent all night with that man!"

"And I spent all night with you," Jill pointed out calmly. "Does that mean that you corrupted me?"

He ran his hand through his hair. "You know what I mean," he said, exasperated.

"I do, but Dillon, they're adults, just like us. And just because she's your mother doesn't mean she can't stay out all night if she wants. And she did forget her key," Jill added for good measure.

"How do you know that wasn't just an excuse?" he wanted to know.

"Do you really think she needs an excuse at her age?" Jill was genuinely puzzled. What was the big deal?

"Yes. No. Oh, I don't know," he complained, dropping his hands and going back to the table for more dishes. "I guess I just don't want to see her get so involved with a man she barely knows."

"If it will ease your mind, I can tell you that I met Bill last week," Jill said. "He's a good man and seems to be good company for your mother. She needs someone her own age to talk to."

"And that's another thing," Dillon said. "Do you really think that's all they did last night? Talk?"

"Do you think they believe that's all we did?" Jill countered with a smile.

"Not for a minute," he said, shaking his head. "But dammit, Jill, that's my mother!"

"I knew that," Jill laughed. "At least you don't have to worry about her getting pregnant at her age."

"Pregnant?! Oh my God!" He hadn't even thought of that.

"Relax, I was just teasing."

She came to stand in front of him. "Don't worry about her." She touched his lips with her fingertips, stopping any comment he was about to make. "Enough about your mother. What about us? Didn't you say you need to go into work today?"

He groaned as he looked at his watch. "Yes, but you made me forget all about it. I'm meeting a couple applying for a loan for their first home," he said, taking her into his arms, "but then I'll have the rest of the weekend free."

A long, leisurely, tantalizing kiss later, it was as if they had never been out of each other's arms, never had the confrontation with his mother.

"This is my Saturday to have Peggy," Jill sighed, reluctant to give up their time alone. "Want to go to the circus again?" She laughed, watching his expression change.

"I want you to know I enjoyed that. Maybe we could," he mused. "I could really develop a taste for cotton candy."

"No, no, not the circus." Jill did not want to go to the circus and she was pretty sure it had moved on to another town. "I was just kidding."

In the end, they decided to take the girls out for pizza, then Dillon went home to change to go into the office.

With Penny still not back, the house seemed unusually quiet. Jill sat down with her tablet and enjoyed a leisurely cup of coffee before the girls got there.

Jill wondered what Dillon was thinking right now, now that they weren't together. She had no regrets, except that she hadn't been able to whisper the words of love that had filled her when their bodies had come together. And that she had heard no such words from Dillon. That was the crux of the whole matter. He said he was ready for marriage, but Jill had to have love. Even Ron had loved her. Maybe not in the way a man should love his wife, but they had shared a love. And they were both young. Neither knew what it was like to feel the heart-stopping, passionate love that Ron had found, and now had found Jill.

But where were they at now? Jill had what she wanted, what she had convinced herself she wanted, a nice casual affair, and a relationship with a man she could talk to. Of course, it wasn't the same as being married, since Dillon wasn't there all night every night, but he had been around every evening. And that would have to do, for now, Jill decided. He apparently was fine with the way it was as well, since he hadn't brought up marriage again.

She got up and rinsed her cup and was tidying the living room when she heard a car pull up. She went to the door to greet Jan and the girls, who were dashing up the sidewalk.

"We're here," Penny shouted.

"Look what we brought you," Peggy added as they stopped in front of Jill. She held out a scraggly bunch of flowers.

Jill knelt to accept them. "How nice of you. Can you go put them in a glass of water so they don't die?"

"Let's go," Penny said turning to Peggy, "we can use the Peppa Pig glass that Grandma Ruth gave me."

Jill straightened again as the girls ran into the house,

letting the door slam behind them. Jan came up the steps to the house, carrying Penny's overnight bag.

"Have fun last night?" Jan asked without any preamble. She handed the bag to Jill.

Jill smiled, giving Jan her answer. There was no need to discuss all the details right now, even if Jill felt like talking about it. The little girls were here, and there would be time later.

"And how about you? Any problems?" Jill asked her sister.

Jan shook her head as the two moved into the living room. She was dressed in a straight black linen skirt, white camisole and black matching jacket. She had a showing before lunch, she told Jill, and then she and Grant were meeting his brother and wife for a game of tennis at the country club. That was as far as she got as the little girls brought the flowers, now resting in a brightly colored glass, back for their mothers to see.

"You can put them on the table by the door and then go play," Jill said, giving Penny a hug.

"All right, but we're hungry."

Peggy nodded her agreement.

"But it's only nine-thirty in the morning," Jill said, smiling. "Didn't you have breakfast this morning?"

"Yes, but we're still hungry," Penny said.

"That figures," Jan said. "You would think they didn't have a seven-course meal an hour ago."

"There's some fruit in the refrigerator," Jill said to the backs of their heads as the girls ran to the kitchen.

"Thanks," they heard them shout as the door swung shut behind them. A few moments later they heard the back door slam.

"Where were we?" Jan asked as the house stopped vibrating. "Oh yes, we might stop for a drink, but we're planning on being home for supper, so we can pick Peggy up."

"When did Richard and Marianne join the country club?" Jill asked. She knew that Jan and Grant didn't belong, Grant preferred to use the university's facilities since he was on staff there.

"Last month. They wanted to play golf today, but Grant talked them out of that, explaining that on Saturday afternoon we would be lucky to get on the course, even if we called ahead for a tee time," Jan said. "And you know, golf is not really my game."

"Mine either," Jill agreed. Well, you can take your time," Jill advised her sister. "We weren't sure what you were doing, so Dillon and I made plans to take the girls out for pizza tonight, if that's all right."

"He wants to take the little girls out for pizza?" Jan asked, shaking her head. "I thought he didn't like kids. So, is he crazy? Or has no idea what he's in for?"

"Probably both. But it was better than a repeat performance at the circus, which is what Dillon voted for."

"Even that's better than golf," Jan said, laughing. "At least he hasn't suggested that."

Neither of the girls particularly cared for golf. "If I'm going for exercise, I want something that will keep me slim," Jan had always said. Jill had gone one step further and actually tried the sport, but had only succeeded in dislocating a shoulder. She had vowed in the doctor's office that day never to step on a golf course again. Even knowing how much Dillon liked golf couldn't change Jill's mind on the subject. Both girls liked tennis. They could play each other and had played in high school.

"I wonder why he hasn't suggested playing golf, now that you mention it," Jill mused. "Not that I would want to, but you know, he hasn't even mentioned golf. Ruth said he spent last weekend playing and he mentioned something about a game this afternoon, but he never suggested I go along."

Jan shrugged, unwilling to guess at an answer and Jill dropped the subject. She wasn't sure she wanted to guess either.

The two chatted for a few more moments before Jan said she needed to get going. "Are you still going to the lake next weekend?" she asked as they walked to the door.

"I think so," Jill replied, "although I almost forgot it was Memorial Day weekend. Are you sure you can't come too?" The cabin, built by the girls' great-grandfather, was located a couple of hours northwest of Minneapolis. It was a great place to spend a weekend. Although it was rented out most of the summer and managed by Jill, the family kept Memorial Day weekend open for themselves. Usually the whole family spent the weekend together there, but this year their parents were going Paula's sister's house in Michigan. Their brother Nance said he other plans but didn't elaborate.

Jan shook her head. "You know we can't back out of going to Grant's class reunion in Wisconsin. We'll have to plan another time."

"I can check the rental schedule," Jill said, "so you guys can get up there at least once this summer."

"The summers go so fast," Jan replied. "Grant's just so busy getting ready for the fall football season, but maybe you and I and the girls can go sometime. See what you have open."

Jill nodded. "I'll do that. And now I should prob-ably should spend some time today doing paperwork. I spent most of the week running around, and I'm getting behind."

After Jan left, Jill headed to her office after making sure the girls were still in the yard. Memorial Day already. Well, she and Penny could go up to the lake. She wanted to check on the cabin anyway and it would be nice to have a break for just the two of them.

****

Dillon stopped short as he entered the country club lounge. His brother nearly bumped into the back of him.

"Hey Dillon, what's up?"

Jill? Here? And talking to Suzanne? He really was dead now.

"What's she doing here?" he asked aloud to one in par-ticular.

"Who, Suzanne?" Jason answered, looking around Dil-lon to where the two women stood with a third, talking. "She's a member, remember?"

"No, I mean the woman she's talking to."

"Yeah, what a looker," Jason gave the two women a long look. "I know the answer is going to be yes, but I have to ask anyway. Do you know her?"

"Yes. No. Not as well as I thought," Dillon finally de-cided. "I would never have taken her for the country-club type."

"Oh yeah? What type would you take her for?" Jason wanted to know. "She looks like she fits into this club just fine. Not to mention that tennis outfit."

She did look good, Dillon conceded. Dressed in all white with her hair pulled up in the messy bun she seemed to prefer, little purple socks and tennis shoes setting off her long tanned legs. Those legs, he remembered so well, entwined with his own only this morning, smooth and silky against his own.

Why hadn't she said something about coming to the club to play tennis? Dillon wondered. He didn't even know she played.

"Hello, are you in there?" Jason was talking to him again. "That's the second time this week I've caught you just staring off into space with that funny look on your face." He paused, considering. "Don't' tell me you're in love?"

"Okay, I won't."

"With the redhead."

"Yeah."

"The one talking to Suzanne."

"Yeah."

"So, it looks as if you have two options," Jason said, grinning widely. It was about time his brother found someone who could turn him into a blithering idiot. "Go talk to them both, or we turn around and get out of here before they spot us. What's your pleasure?"

"I guess we go talk to them," Dillon said, grimacing, "since they just spotted us. Coming?"

"Sure. I wouldn't miss this for the world."

"Hi Dillon, Jason, where's Meredith?" Suzanne greeted them as the men approached.

"She had a party of some sort to go to this afternoon," Jason answered. "A baby shower, I think. She took Ben with her."

Dillon was watching Jill. She seemed very relaxed, and it puzzled him until Suzanne spoke again.

"Jan, Marianne, this is Dillon and Jason Hanley." Suzanne introduced the women, allowing Dillon to breathe evenly again. Jan. He had forgotten about Jan. And now that he was closer, he could tell she wasn't Jill. It was hard to explain, but her eyes weren't the same, they weren't as soft as they had been that morning.

"And this is Jan Humphrey and her sister-in-law Marianne Humphrey," Suzanne was saying. "I do accounting for Jan's sister. You would be surprised how much Jill looks like Jan."

Dillon would believe it. His moment of relief was over, Dillon thought as everyone shook hands. No wonder Jill knew about the blondes, she had talked to one of them. He was probably lucky she hadn't belted him. Maybe they hadn't talked about him, since Suzanne still seemed friendly.

"I've met Dillon," Jan told Suzanne. "Did you know his mother lives next door to Jill?"

Suzanne looked at Dillon, raising her eyebrows. "Is that right? How interesting."

"Very interesting," Jason echoed, thinking he might have to pay his mother a visit. It appeared he was missing out on too many things.

"So, you've met Jill too?" Suzanne asked.

She sounded suspicious, Dillon thought. He hoped it was his imagination.

"Um, yes, as a matter of fact," he answered, trying to regain control of the situation without giving himself away. "She invited Mom and I to a barbecue a couple of weeks ago." Casual. That was the answer. Just be casual, Hanley.

"Where's Grant today?" he asked Jan, hoping to change the subject. It apparently worked as Jan explained the men were holding a table for them on the patio. Marianne piped in about a bridge party she was planning in several weeks. Dillon and Jason listened politely, then made their good-byes and after finding an empty table, sat and ordered a couple of beers.

"So, tell me all about this Jill," Jason said conversationally after they received their drinks. "Lives next door to Mom, huh? I bet she set you up, didn't she?"

"Mom had nothing to do with it. Or very little," Dillon amended, since he wouldn't have met Jill if she didn't live where she did. He was almost convinced that Ruth actually hadn't been matchmaking, she was too involved in her own romance right now.

"So, is it serious?" Jason asked jokingly.

"Of course not," Dillon said, crossing his fingers under the table. If he told Jason just how special Jill was to him, his mother and the whole town would know in about five minutes. Jason was a good brother, but he never could keep a secret.

Dillon remembered the time he and Jason went skinny-dipping in the Minnesota River with several girls when they were young. They had managed to keep their clothes dry and no one would have ever been the wiser, except that Jason had bragged about it. Word eventually gotten back to their parents, who were not happy when they discovered their sons had not only skinny-dipped, which was bad enough, but they had done so in the company of young ladies, whose parents had also found out and were blaming the boys.

In Jill's case, Dillon wanted Jill to be the first to know

just how he felt. He didn't want to scare her off by spreading rumors that he was in love. He decided he just didn't want the world to know until he was sure of Jill's feelings.

Now that they had slept together, Dillon was sure that Jill felt something for him, but was it enough for marriage? He guessed they now had what Jill termed her 'casual affair,' since he couldn't resist her, but he was convinced more than ever that his love was real. Now he just had to convince Jill. It didn't matter that marriage wasn't in the cards for today, he decided, because he had time to wait, but that time would be precious if Jason caught on.

"It was just a barbecue," Dillon continued. "And Mom was there too, as well as the Humphreys."

"But you have seen her since, haven't you?" Jason said, taking a drink of his beer.

"Okay, I took her out to dinner one night and we went to a play together last night," Dillon admitted, seeing where Jason's questioning was leading. If he said he hadn't seen her since, then Jason would really get suspicious.

"So what's she look like?" Jason asked.

Dillon pointed to the women walking out of the room. "That," he said.

"She looks like her sister?" Jason asked.

Dillon nodded. "Exactly like her," he clarified. "They aren't twins but they easily could be. Jan is older but not by much." He decided it was time to change the subject back to his mother.

"So, how do you know that they spent the night together?" Jason asked, when Dillon finished filling him in on the latest developments.

"Well . . . I happened to go over there early this morning," Dillon said, "but that's not the point. I think she's really interested in this guy."

"So, what's wrong with that?" Jason shrugged. "As long as he's not after her money, what difference does it make? Do you think that's what he's interested in?" he asked, sitting a little straighter.

"No, I don't think so," Dillon growled into his beer. "I think he's after her body," he said, causing Jason to laugh heartily at his glaring look.

****

"I think he's after my body."

Ruth and Jill were sharing Ruth's porch swing, drinking sodas and watching Penny and Peggy race across the yard. Jill had worked diligently for several hours, only stopping to fix lunch and occasionally remind the girls to stay in the yard when they came in to ask her when lunch would be ready, or if they could visit Grandma Ruth, or things like why butterflies had wings. They had finally gotten out their tablets to watch videos while Jill finished up.

Now she felt like she was prepared for the upcoming week and could enjoy the rest of the weekend, beginning with this chance to sit and relax for a few moments. She had a little time before she needed to start getting the girls ready for their evening, and decided they needed to get rid of a little energy.

She tried not to choke on her soda she digested Ruth's statement, holding in a laugh. "And that makes you happy?"

"Oh yes," Ruth sighed. "Bill is so handsome and he makes me feel so young. And he wouldn't be near as interesting if he were only interested in my mind. I'll still have that, I hope, when my body's long given up."

Jill couldn't help it. She laughed out loud. "Ruth, you are such a dear," she said, patting Ruth's arm. "How did I ever get lucky enough to get you for a neighbor?"

"I don't know, but tell me about Dillon and you," she insisted. "How was your evening?"

"It was nice," Jill answered, taking a sip of her soda and hoping Ruth didn't notice the heat reddening her face. Nice? Naughty was more like it. A wonderfully, naughty night, one she wouldn't be forgetting any time soon.

"Nice?" Ruth harrumphed. "I've known my son all his life and I don't think he's ever shown a date a 'nice' time. Especially if they're still together at breakfast."

"Okay," Jill admitted, "it was terrific."

"That's more like it." Ruth nodded, satisfied. "And I'm sure you didn't talk all night like Bill and I did."

"How do I know you two just talked?" Jill said, turning the tables. "You just said Bill was after your body."

"I said he was after it," she sniffed. "I didn't say he got it."

Jill laughed again, unable to help herself and Ruth joined in.

"Seriously, Jill," the older woman said, "Dillon is my son and I love him dearly, but I've come to love you too, and I can't sit by and let him hurt you."

"He won't hurt me, I assure you," Jill protested, but Ruth was shaking her head.

"He told me he's decided he's ready for marriage," she continued, "and that you are going to be his wife. No, no, don't say anything yet," Ruth said as Jill opened her mouth to speak, "I'm sure he thinks that's what he wants, and I know I would just love having you as a daughter-in-law, but I think he needs to be certain of his feelings before he rushes into marriage. Do you understand what I'm trying to say?" she asked, placing Jill's hand in her own.

Jill nodded sadly. "Yes, because it's what I thought myself."

"You deserve to have a man who loves you, and while I'm sure Dillon cares a great deal for you, he's never been in love before," Ruth said. "I'm not sure he knows the meaning of love. Oh darn, I've made you sad," she added, noting the look on the younger woman's face. "Let's talk about something else. Penny tells me you and she are going to spend next weekend at a lake somewhere."

"We are," Jill replied, sounding disappointed. "It was supposed to be a weekend to spend with my whole family but everyone canceled. We're still going to go, but it won't be the same without them."

****

Jill thought about the afternoon's conversation as Dillon took her and Penny home that evening. The little girls had a wonderful time at the pizza parlor and they had already taken Peggy home. Now that Penny was dozing in the back seat, Jill had little to say. Ruth's words ran over and over through her mind, but only because they confirmed her own thoughts. She appreciated the older woman's concern, even if it caused her heart to ache.

Jill tried to tell herself that she had asked for this relationship, so if she got hurt it was no one's fault but her own. She wasn't expecting marriage, and she had told Dillon that. He hadn't mentioned it again, so everything was fine. Wasn't it? Yes!

"Jill?"

"What?" Jill shouted as she jumped in her seat, startled.

"Shh, you'll wake Penny," he cautioned, glancing behind him. "I just wanted to know what's wrong with you tonight." He had mentioned meeting Jan at the country club but hadn't mentioned that she had been talking to Suzanne Hall, his regular golfing and dinner partner. At least she had been until he met Jill. Could it be that Jan had already told her sister of the meeting and the fact that he knew Suzanne? Dillon wanted to tell her himself, let her know that Suzanne was just a friend, not competition.

"Nothing. Nothing is wrong, I had a wonderful evening. I'm just a little tired, you know how having two little girls around all day can wear you out." Oh Lord, she was babbling. Jill lapsed into silence.

Dillon knew something definitely wrong as the silence in the car lengthened, but he wasn't sure what to say. Just the fact that Jill had been babbling was enough to tell him something was wrong. Jill never babbled. She was calm even when a normal adult was reduced to tears, like when in the middle of a pizza parlor, one six-year-old dropped her pizza on the floor and the other spilled soft drink all over the waitress. And how about when one announced loudly to the entire room that she had to go to the bathroom? Dillon chuckled softly, remembering.

"What?" Jill asked suspiciously, glancing at him. She hadn't, and wasn't, going to tell him about her conversation with his mother, deciding it would serve no purpose.

"I was just thinking about Penny's announcement this evening," he said, hoping to ease the tension in the air.

It worked as Jill joined his quiet laughter, mindful of the sleeping child. "It could have been worse, you know."

"It could have been worse?"

"Sure. She could have announced that you had to use the men's room," Jill explained. "Not quite that nicely, mind you. Or one of them could have thrown up all over the floor. That's happened before."

Dillon groaned in understanding. "I suppose I should be thankful for small favors then."

The more pleasant mood prevailed the rest of the ride back to Jill's, as she pushed all depressing thoughts out of her mind.

For now, she should be content with the relationship, and she was, Jill told herself later as Dillon gave her a long, spine-shivering, sock-knocking-off kiss to end the evening. It wasn't nearly enough to satisfy either one's desire, but it would have to hold them, they decided, for a more opportune time. Penny was asleep in the next room, Jill reminded Dillon. Ruth's light was still on, Dillon added disgustedly.

"She didn't say anything to me when I called her earlier today about what we did all night," he said as they stood near the door, arms entwined in a familiar embrace, "and do you know what that means?"

His mother had simply smiled and nodded when he had announced his intentions with Jill, which made him suspicious all over again. She hadn't even asked any questions on why all of a sudden he had changed his mind. Was it possible he was being set up, by his own mother, a pro at the art of matchmaking?

"I haven't a clue." Except that she talked to me, Jill thought.

"It means that she's decided to keep us on our toes," he said. "Anyway, I'm going to stop over when I leave here to check on her."

"It's nice that you two are close," Jill said as she walked him to the door. A kiss to the cheek and he was gone. It was probably for the best, Jill thought. This way there was less temptation.

****

Dillon called after Sunday lunch.

"Are you busy?" he asked when Jill answered.

"Penny and I are just doing laundry," she replied. "Aren't you golfing?" She was pretty certain he usually played golf on Sunday afternoons.

"No," Dillon answered. He wasn't sure why he even called her. He should be golfing, spending time with his brother. "I was just thinking we could do something this afternoon."

"Sure," Jill answered, turning on the dryer. "What do you have in mind?"

Penny was jumping up and down. "Is that Dillon? Can I talk to him? Is he coming over? I want to show him the picture I drew today."

Jill put her finger to her lips. "Just a minute, Penny," she cautioned, but there was silence on the phone.

"Hello?" she asked. "Are you still there? Dillon?"

What did he have in mind? Oh yeah. His place, his bed, just the two of them, all afternoon, no mothers, no children. Children. Penny. "I'm here," he said.

"Do you know I can almost see you leering at me through the phone?" she asked, laughing.

His body tightened.

"Something public," he murmured, unaware that he

was speaking out loud.

She raised her eyebrows. "Public?"

"I may have been leering but that wasn't what I was thinking, so behave yourself," he returned, huskily. "Do you play golf?" he asked before he realized the implications of the question.

If they played golf, they would be at the club, and would risk running into Suzanne. Well, how bad could that be? They already knew each other, after all. It could be disastrous.

Jill stiffened. It was the dreaded question, rating right up there with how well she liked pro baseball. She did not.

"No."

"No, you don't play golf, or no, you won't behave?"

"No, I don't play golf. Have you ever played golf with a six-year-old traipsing around after you, asking twenty questions?"

"She only asks you twenty questions? I get at least thirty, maybe forty when I'm with her," he said, almost relieved with her answer.

Jill laughed, glad that he had accepted her explanation so easily. Dislocating her shoulder playing golf was not something she wanted anyone to know about. Even Dillon. Especially Dillon. Even after all these years, it was still one of her most embarrassing experiences, rating up there with pitching a bowling ball into the crowd of boys behind her when she was in high school.

"What about miniature golf?" he asked. "It's a beautiful afternoon and Penny would love it, don't you think?"

Jill acknowledged both of those things and turned to Penny.

"Do you want to go golfing with Dillon?" she asked.

She was rewarded with a shout and after Jill confirmed it would be fine, they hung up.

Penny tugged on her sleeve. "Mom, what's golf?" she asked, leaving Jill smiling.

Chapter 8

Penny loved miniature golf.

Jill enjoyed it, but she wasn't sure Dillon did. Up until now he had been with both Penny and Peggy in a mostly controlled environment. Penny was well-behaved but still a six-year-old and she acted like a six-year-old, running ahead and back, then ahead again. She fell and skinned both her knees, which made her cry inconsolably. Dillon was clearly embarrassed and didn't know what to do. He finally picked her up and held her close until she stopped crying.

Jill's heart melted.

He may not like children but Penny liked him. Loved him, Jill would guess. She could not stop talking about him when they got home that night.

It continued throughout the week. Jill took Penny with her when she went to clients' homes and the little girl played with her dolls while her mother worked in the office. Through it all, it was Dillon this and Dillon that. She and Dillon had only talked a couple of times on the phone, he was busy at work and went home each night without stopping by.

Jill admitted she missed him. Talking to him on the phone wasn't the same as seeing him. She wondered why he was staying away and concluded the miniature golfing experience had sent him back to the country club.

She shrugged thinking about it as she straightened the house Wednesday afternoon. They were leaving for the lake Friday afternoon so she wanted to get her house in order. They had already gone grocery shopping. Penny was so excited she couldn't stop bouncing.

Jill was surprised when he stopped by that evening. Dillon knew they were going to the lake for the weekend. He didn't ask to tag along and she didn't mention it again.

Penny met him at the door, hugging his knees. Jill followed her daughter.

"Guess what, Dillon?" Penny asked. "We're going to the lake."

Dillon hefted her into his arms. "That's what I hear," he said. "Are you excited?"

Penny nodded. "I am sooo excited," she said. "Do you want to come along? It's fun at the lake."

"I don't think..." Dillon started to speak.

"Penny, I think Dillon might have other plans for the weekend," Jill interrupted. "I'm sure he doesn't want to spend the weekend with us at a little cabin on a lake."

Dillon looked at Jill and then at Penny who was waiting impatiently for his answer.

"As a matter of fact, I don't have any plans for the weekend," he said. "I'd love to come, if it's okay with your mom." His only plans included a couple rounds of golf with Jason but this sounded like much more fun. He had missed them both during the week and wanted to spend time with them. If they were okay with it, he was in.

"Is it Mom? Is it?" Penny asked.

Now they both looked at Jill and she melted. He looked so good holding her little girl and he treated her so well.

"Well...." Jill started.

Penny wiggled out of Dillon's arms to jump up and down. "Yay," she shouted.

"Just a minute Penny," Jill said. "Are you sure you want to come along, Dillon? It's not very exciting."

Dillon nodded. He couldn't think of anything he would like more except maybe to scoop them both up right now and hug them both.

"Okay, then," Jill said. "He can come along." She turned to Dillon. "We're leaving Friday after lunch and we don't take dress up, we just wear jeans and t-shirts."

He nodded. "Got it," he said. "What about food?"

"Bring what you want," Jill said. "We have food we can grill, like hamburgers and hot dogs, easy things to take and cook." She went over their menu for the weekend and they discussed when they were leaving.

"Sounds good to me," he replied. "I'll add a few things to that. And I can drive if you like."

Jill nodded.

"Can we go golfing again?" Penny asked hopefully. "Now?"

"It's almost bedtime for you, Missy," Jill said, shaking her head. "Go get on your pajamas and maybe Dillon will read to you."

Penny was gone in a flash.

"Is that okay?" Jill asked.

Dillon assured her he was fine with reading and was true to his word. The three of them snuggled on the sofa and Dillon read at least four stories until Penny's eyes drooped closed. He rose with her in his arms and carried her to bed.

Jill tucked her in and they went back to the living room. "Would you like something to drink?" she asked him.

He declined, saying he would be back on Friday. He needed to have an early night so he could get his work done before they left. He also was trying to keep a physical distance, just to assure her he wasn't interested in an affair with her. It almost worked as they met as one at the door. The kiss was long and deep and when they broke apart, they were both breathing heavily.

"I've got to go," Dillon said, his voice husky. "I'll see you Friday."

"How about dinner tomorrow night?" she asked, her own voice a little unsteady. "We're having spaghetti."

"I like spaghetti," he replied, giving her a kiss on the cheek. "I'll see you tomorrow night."

After he left, Jill wandered back to the sofa. "Whew," she said out loud, reliving the kiss. "It's going to be a long night."

It was a long night. Jill couldn't get to sleep and then she couldn't stay asleep, thinking about kisses and why all of a sudden Dillon seemed to be backing away from her. She didn't understand what he wanted out of their relationship. She didn't even kmow what she wanted out of this relationship.

****

"Yoo hoo," Ruth called from Jill's front porch the next afternoon. "Are you home?"

"Come in Ruth," Jill responded from the kitchen. "We're making cookies."

Penny bounced through the kitchen door to greet the older woman. "Come look at our cookies," she said, happily. "You can have one if you want."

"Why thanks, Penny," she replied, taking one from the table where the chocolate chip cookies were cooling. "What's the occasion?"

Jill set a pan of cookies in the oven to bake and got Ruth a cup from the cupboard. "Coffee?" she asked.

Ruth nodded as Penny started talking.

"We're going to the lake tomorrow and we like to take

cookies with us," the little girl explained. She turned to her mother. "Mom, we should invite Grandma Ruth to go with us too."

Ruth raised her eyebrows. "Too?" she asked. "Who else is going? Peggy?"

Penny shook her head. "Dillon is coming," she said. "You can come too, can't she, Mom?"

Jill smiled. "We would love to have your company," she replied to Ruth. "We're leaving tomorrow afternoon and coming back on Monday."

Ruth thought about it for a moment. "Oh," she said, "I couldn't possibly spend the whole weekend there. Bill is helping with the Memorial Day services at the cemetery on Monday. I told him I would go with him."

Jill remembered Bill was a veteran. She nodded. "Maybe you could come on Saturday for the day," she suggested. "The weather's supposed to be nice."

Ruth shook her head. "I couldn't possibly drive all that way with this brace," she replied. "but thanks for asking."

Penny piped up. "Maybe Bill could drive you," she offered. "I like Bill, and he could come too. Could he come too, Mom?"

Jill saw no way out of this. "That would work," she said. She had no idea what Dillon would say about this, but it was going to be an interesting weekend. Dillon was still not fond of Bill, but maybe if they all spent the day together Dillon might warm up to the older man.

"Are you sure?" Ruth asked. "Let me check with Bill." She pulled out her phone and called him, gave him the details.

From the smile on Ruth's face, Jill guessed Bill's response was an emphatic 'yes.'

"He wants to know if there's fishing," Ruth relayed to Jill.

Jill nodded. "The best. We won't have a boat but there is a dock he can fish off of."

Ruth repeated the information to the man on the other end of the phone and after a short pause, smiled.

"Apparently, we're spending Saturday at the lake," Ruth said. "Bill is so excited. He hasn't been fishing all spring so this will be a treat. He's going to teach me to fish."

Plans were made and that was the easy part, Jill thought. The hard part would be telling Dillon. She was pretty sure he would be fine with Ruth tagging along, but Bill? He still wasn't a big fan of Bill and it could make for a tense day.

Surprisingly, Dillon was fine with the new arrangement. They talked about the trip over spaghetti, with Penny interjecting her plans for playing at the lake. Her bright kinks of hair shook as she discussed looking for treasures at the lake, from feathers to rocks.

"Will you help me find rocks?" she asked Dillon as they finished dinner.

"Of course I will," Dillon replied. He was surprised how much he was looking forward to it. Bill Weaver aside, the weekend held promise. He was equally surprised that he was looking forward to hunting rocks with a six-year-old girl with the craziest, brightest hair he had ever seen. For a guy who proclaimed he didn't like children, he was totally enamored with this one.

It was already dark and Penny was tucked in bed when Dillon decided it was time to head home. He didn't want to give his mother any more ideas than she already had. Jill walked him to the front door where he looked over to her house to see if she was watching through a window. He would stop over and tell her goodnight.

"Any sign of Ruth?" Jill asked, catching the direction of

his glance.

He shook his head.

"She's probably out in the bushes right now, watching us to see if I'm going to stay all night," he said.

Jill burst into giggles at the thought of Ruth Hanley crouched in the bushes, waiting for evidence that her son and his date were doing something improper. Really. This man didn't know his mother at all.

"Okay, maybe not in the bushes, but you get the picture," he relented, caressing her cheek with his fingers.

"I get the picture," she said drawing in her breath. It amazed her how they could go from teasing laughter one moment to sensual awareness the next, Jill thought as he claimed her lips.

"I wonder if I could get her to bake an apple pie to bring along," Dillon said as they stepped apart.

"Is that what you're thinking about?" Jill asked, giving him a quick kiss on the lips, "I think it's a wonderful idea." She turned him toward the door. "You can ask her when you go by the bushes."

She laughed and Dillon couldn't resist a smile of his own.

Dillon heard voices whispering as soon as he stepped out the door, but he couldn't make out what they were saying. Was that his mother? No, it couldn't be. Even he wouldn't believe that she would actually be lurking in the bushes waiting to see when he was leaving Jill's house.

He put his hands in his pockets and started down the steps, whistling. The voices had stopped when the door shut, so he didn't give it much thought, his mind on Jill and her delicious kisses. How he wished he could spend the night. He sighed. Someday he would. Dillon stepped off the sidewalk to cut across to the corner of Ruth's fence. He didn't notice the shadowed figure straightening up from the ground until he smacked into it, nearly knocking both of them to the ground.

"What the . . . ?" Dillon steadied himself by clutching at the intruder's arms. Could it be his mother? Of course not, it must be a burglar. Dillon tensed his body in anticipation of a fight, only to halt a moment later as he recognized the voice in the darkness.

"Don't you ever pay attention to what you're doing?" came the exasperated reply. "I tell you son, that's really going to get you into trouble one of these days."

"Mother?"

"Of course it's me," Ruth answered indignantly, straightening her glasses as Bill appeared next to her. He wielded a flashlight and a small bucket. Dillon covered his eyes with his hand as the light caught him across the face.

"Would you get that thing out of my face?" Dillon demanded. "And tell me what you're doing out here, lurking in the bushes?"

"Dillon Hanley!" his mother admonished, puffing out like a wounded bird. "I have never lurked in my life and I'm not about to start now!"

"Actually," Bill Weaver put in amicably, "we're looking for nightcrawlers."

"Worms?"

"Yes. We're going to need some bait for our fishing trip Saturday," the older man explained, holding up the bucket and splaying the light on the slippery worms. "Jill left her sprinkler on earlier and it brought the crawlers right out of the ground. Best place to get them is right under these bushes. You know, they make the best bait, and they're easier to handle than minnows. I think they work better than lures."

"Worms?" Dillon repeated, shaking his head.

"That's right young man, and next time you try to run someone over, I hope you'll wait for an explanation before you start accusing them of lurking," his mother said, shaking her finger at him.

"I . . ."

"What's going on out here?" Jill asked from the porch. She had opened the door and was coming out of the house.

"He accused us of lurking," Ruth Hanley got in before the men could speak. "My own son."

"Lurking? You don't say." Jill raised her eyebrows at Dillon, who had turned around and was facing her along with the other two. She tried not to laugh.

"This is not funny, Baxter," Dillon warned.

"And he scared off all off the nightcrawlers," Bill added, muttering to himself. "I hope we have enough."

"Would you forget about the damn worms?" Dillon exploded, catching the other man's words.

"There is no need to swear," Ruth reminded her son. "After all, we were just minding our own business out here."

It was happening again, Dillon thought, running his fingers through his hair. He was losing control over the situation. And it was all Jill's fault. Ever since he had met her, Dillon had been finding himself in the middle of these bizarre conversations. At the bank he was always in control. At the club too. What had happened here tonight? All he did was walk out of her house. It shouldn't matter that he had his mind on Jill instead of his walking, he had been walking for most of his life. She was a distraction, no doubt about it. But oh, what a sweet distraction, Dillon thought, thinking about the time she spent in his arms.

"Actually, the worms are a good idea," Jill said, coming

down the steps and shaking Dillon from his reverie. "Dillon was supposed to be on his way over to your house Ruth, to ask if you would make an apple pie for Saturday." She smiled mischievously.

"I can do that," Ruth said. "We certainly don't want to come empty-handed. And I don't think nightcrawlers count," Ruth said to Jill.

Bill nodded hesitantly. "We were thinking we should bring something along besides worms. They just don't agree with my stomach like they used to," he said.

Jill nodded, laughing. "Of course."

"Dillon?" his mother said.

"What?" he shouted, causing the other three to jump.

"There's no need to shout," Ruth told him, holding her hands against her chest. "One of these days you're really going to give me a heart attack." She turned to the others, sadly shaking her head. "I thought I raised my boys not to act like this, but evidently I went wrong somewhere."

"I understand completely," Jill commiserated, imagining the shock Dillon must have gotten only a few moments ago when he discovered his mother actually was outside her house.

"All I wanted to know was if our coming along was all right with you, Dillon," Ruth added to her son.

"Yes, of course it is. I guess," he added under his breath, looking at Jill again. She just smiled.

"Come on Ruth, let's go take care of these worms," Bill suggested, eager to be gone. He wasn't in the mood to wrestle with Ruth's son again.

They said their goodnights. As the couple started off across the lawn, Bill and Ruth's voices drifted back to her. They were discussing Dillon's sanity and whether it was indeed safe to go anywhere with him, and the bewildered look on Dillon's face made Jill laugh again.

"Go home, Hanley," she advised, going to Dillon and guiding him to his car. "You need a good night's rest."

He didn't bother to comment on that, knowing that rest and sleep were two of the last things he needed, but waited until he was alone in the car and heading down the street.

"I think I need a drink," he muttered, "or maybe a straight jacket."

****

"Row, row, row your boat..."

"Row, row, row your boat..."

Penny led the adults in a round for the fifteenth time on their journey Friday afternoon.

It was about a two-hour drive and Dillon was rethinking spending the whole weekend with a six-year-old. They already had to stop twice for bathroom breaks and then she was hungry. Or thirsty. Or bored.

Dillon had a long talk with himself when he got home the night before. He wasn't going crazy. And from now on, he was in control. He was calling the shots. At least, he amended, he was going to pay more attention to the conversations around him. No more focusing only on Jill and her tempting body. He wouldn't touch her. He wouldn't look at her. He probably shouldn't even be in the same vehicle with her. Of course, with Penny along and his mother and Bill coming tomorrow, it shouldn't be too hard to find something else to keep his attention. All three made good chaperones.

He would have preferred to be alone with Jill but he supposed real life wasn't like that. Having his mother come along was an adjustment and having Bill drive her made sense. It wasn't that Dillon disliked the man. He supposed now that he had gotten used to the idea of his mother seeing someone, Bill was as good as anyone. Bill Weaver seemed to make her happy, Dillon just wasn't sure he wanted to double date with his mother.

Dillon resigned himself to a group outing. Who would have thought a month ago that Dillon Hanley, reputed bachelor, would be going on a family outing, complete with children and old people? He hoped this wasn't a sign of things to come, like a mini van.

He would have to touch Jill, Dillon decided minutes later, glancing over and meeting her eyes as Penny started the song again, despite the resolutions he had just made. He wanted to kiss her right there in his pickup.

Stop it Hanley, he steadied himself, you'll drive off the road. He turned his attention back to the road, but his mind still wandered. Maybe they could sneak off behind a bush. He would have to work on that he decided as the round finished and Penny began suggesting other songs to sing.

****

The cabin was rustic, Dillon decided, but in a charming way. The main living area and kitchen were one long room with patio doors opening to a covered front porch that spanned the front of the house. A fireplace took up the wall opposite the kitchen and the walls were knotty pine. A sofa and several comfortable chairs made a cozy place to look out onto the lake. It was steps to the lake and a long dock that jutted out into the water. Overlooking the rock-strewn beach of the glacial lake, the cabin was surrounded by huge pines.

It offered a cool place to spend a weekend or the whole summer, Dillon thought.

Jill took one of the two bedrooms for her and Penny, leaving the other for Dillon.

Dillon took the news that they would be in separate bedrooms with good grace. It was important, Jill thought, that Penny understand Dillon wasn't here to monopolize her mother. They could all snuggle together on the sofa, Jill decided, and it would be like they were a real family. No. She would be wise to remember they were not a family and she needed to remember Ruth's words. Dillon was not a family man. He didn't want a family.

Dillon was good company and truly seemed fond of Penny, Jill thought. He said he wanted her, said he wanted to marry her. He had backed off talking about that, though, so maybe he had decided for a more casual relationship. It was her worst fear. She didn't want Penny hurt, and she sure didn't want her own heart broken.

They spent the evening outdoors. Dillon grilled hamburgers and they had a feast with chips and salad and fresh vegetables. Later, Jill and Dillon sat on the dock with Penny, watching the sunset.

It was truly breathtaking here, Dillon decided. "I'm surprised you don't live out here all year," he said. "It's spectacular."

Jill shook her head. "It's not practical," she answered. "My business is hands-on and Penny's school is just a few blocks from our house. It's too far to commute and we would be at the mercy of the weather during the winter months."

Dillon understood, but he could easily see the three of them living here, spending long summer days and cold winter nights here. There were a number of docks that jutted out from the shore up and down the lake's edge, showing that there were many cabins here, but the thick stands of trees hid them from sight, making it seem very private. He shook his head. What was he thinking? He had a life in Mankato and Jill was right, it was too far to commute.

"How long have you owned this place?" he asked, looking back at the cabin.

"All my life," Jill answered. "I think it was built in the early 1900s as a one-room cabin by my great-grandfather and passed down through my mom's family, but Mom and Dad expanded it over the years. It originally had no indoor plumbing and no electricity."

Plumbing was definitely a good addition, Dillon agreed, as was electricity.

"We used to come out here often when were young, but we all went our separate ways," Jill explained. "Mom and Dad come out occasionally, and my brother uses the cabin quite a bit. We all try to come out for Memorial Day and Labor Day but it's harder with everyone so busy."

Jill did like it here. Especially when the man beside her was here too. Maybe they should come more often.

****

"This is great," Bill boomed as Jill and Dillon helped unload his pickup. "I sure am glad we got all those crawlers, there should be some great fishing here."

Dillon found the guy was growing on him, even if he was a little rough around the edges for his taste. Bill was nothing like Ruth's first husband. He was loud and for every story someone told, Bill had six better stories to tell. Today he wore baggy blue jeans and a faded cotton button-up shirt with the sleeves rolled up.

Jill could tell that Dillon wasn't quite as pleased having Bill along as he had been when they were making plans. Of course, inviting Bill Weaver along hadn't been his idea. From the way he shuddered when Bill mentioned the nightcrawlers, it was a good bet that Dillon wasn't interested in fishing.

"I bet the hunting here is pretty good in the winter too," Bill was saying, smiling broadly and making Dillon shudder again. He admitted that Bill seemed good for his mother and was probably a good guy all the way around, but Dillon still could not bring himself to embrace the man. He obviously liked the outdoors, which was fine with Dillon, but for some reason anything involving dead animals held little appeal for him personally.

It probably had something to do with the dead raccoon Dillon had discovered in his bed when he was about ten, courtesy of Jason. Even now Dillon cold easily picture the bloated body of the animal, its beady eyes staring at him from its place on the sheets of his bed and Jason laughing uproariously from his own bed across the room. He could still feel the fur on his leg and hear his own screams as he realized there was something in his bed.

But it was the last practical joke Jason had ever played on him, Dillon reflected, because the next night when Jason got in bed, he got a taste of his own medicine. Dillon had scattered sugar on his sheets, because he wasn't about to resort to dead animals, and he had collected several hundred ants for good measure. Of course, both boys had gotten spankings, but the whole incident had engraved itself firmly in Dillon's mind. Nope, no dead animals for him.

Lunch was a boisterous affair, with everyone stuffing themselves on Ruth's fried chicken and Jill's potato salad.

They also had rolls and Ruth's apple pie, as well as a large bowl of fruit. After the last crumbs were cleaned off the picnic table on the long front porch, Bill collected his fishing gear and took Ruth and Penny down to the shore to try their luck.

"How about you?" Jill asked as they stood on the porch steps and watched the other three walk away. "There are a couple more fishing poles in the cabin, we could see if there really are any bass in this lake."

"Um..." How could he tell her he had never cared for fishing, even living in a great fishing state like Minnesota? It might be okay if he could sit with his line in the water and never catch one so he didn't have to touch the fish. "I'm not really much of a fisherman," he finally said. "Golf is more my speed."

"We can sit in our lawn chairs and watch the fishing," Jill suggested. "I've got cold drinks."

Dillon nodded. Why not? As long as they didn't ask him to assist. They settled in and enjoyed the antics of the three fishing. Dillon had a hunch that Bill was a serious fisherman and not used to a six-year-old jumping up and down as he pulled one in. The whole dock was bouncing and Bill nearly lost his fish, his footing and his dignity.

Dillon and Jill laughed. This was a great way to spend a Saturday afternoon.

It wasn't long before Penny caught her own fish. Bill patiently helped her reel it in, the little girl too excited to turn the crank.

"Mom, Mom," she shouted. "Look, I caught a fish, I caught a fish." She took the pole and the fish from Bill and ran back to Jill and Dillon. "It's a real fish," Penny said, "and I caught it. All by myself."

"You sure did," Jill acknowledged. "Let's take your picture."

Jill took out her phone and snapped a picture of her daughter with her six-inch fish.

"Look, Dillon, I caught a fish." Penny swung around to Dillon, nearly hitting him in the head with the fish. He ducked just in time.

"Maybe you should take the fish back to Bill so he can put it back in the lake," Jill told her daughter, who ran back down the dock to the older couple.

Jill laughed and turned to Dillon. He looked stricken. Her grin faded.

"What's wrong?" she asked.

Dillon shook his head and told her the story about the raccoon. "It probably seems silly to you, but I really don't like dead animals."

Jill was surprised by the revelation, but she didn't find it silly. It showed a different side of him. Dillon was a large man, with fantastic muscles who looked like hunting and fishing would be second nature to him, and he didn't like dead animals. It was sweet, but she wasn't going to tell him that. She also wasn't going to tell him the fish Penny was swinging around on her pole wasn't dead.

Jill took them snacks and drinks, but Penny was so engrossed by the new experience, she didn't get bored.

By the time the three called it quits, it was nearing dinnertime. Bill took over the cooking duties and was grilling hot dogs and a couple of steaks when the cabin door opened.

He looked up at Dillon as the younger man came out of the cabin and sat in a deck chair facing the lake.

Bill gestured toward the western sky. "Looks like a storm might be brewing," he said. "I think Ruth and I should leave as soon as dinner is over so we can get back to town."

Dillon looked out over the lake. Clouds were building off to the west. He checked the weather on his phone. Bill was right, a storm was coming in from the southwest. He showed Bill.

"I agree," Dillon said. "It looks like it could get bad."

****

The storm moved in sooner than they anticipated and with vengeance.

Bill and Ruth were loading their belongings into Bill's pickup when the first crack of lightning hit, followed by a loud clap of thunder and large spatters of rain.

Jill herded everyone back into the cabin. Another flash of lightning and a clap of thunder shook the cabin.

"You're going to have to wait it out," she told the older couple. "You can't drive in this."

Dillon agreed. He didn't want his mother out in this, he thought as the rain lashed against the windows. "Unless it blows over quickly, you're going to have to spend the night." He hated making the suggestion but it was the only thing to do. The lights flickered with another flash of lightning and then the cabin went dark.

"Uh oh, there went the 'tricity," Penny announced. It was something that happened from time to time. Jill was glad Penny wasn't scared by storms. She was too interested in them.

Bill offered to start a fire in the fireplace and Ruth found some candles in a drawer. Jill got the old barn lantern off of the fireplace mantle. Soon they had light and the fire crackled, warming the room.

Jill found a deck of cards and they spent the evening playing Crazy Eights with Penny, who giggled every time she was able to play an eight and change the suit.

Dillon popped popcorn for them in the fireplace and won Penny's heart forever. She was mesmerized by the process.

"I think it's time for bed for you, young lady," Jill finally told Penny. The lights flicked on and added light came from the kitchen and two lamps in the living room. She took the little girl to the bedroom and helped her put on pajamas. They had found a cot in the closet for Penny to sleep on and she was asleep before Jill finished covering her with a blanket.

Ruth and Jill were sharing the bedroom with Penny. Dillon was staying in the second bedroom he had used last night and Bill insisted he take the foldout sofa in the living room.

"I can sleep just about anywhere," he claimed. "Once, I slept in a barn with three cows, a horse and several chickens. After I got out of the service, I worked for a farmer in the northern part of the state. The first winter I was there, we had a blizzard that lasted three days. You couldn't see the house from the barn and when I got done doing chores, I couldn't make it back to the house. So I used a couple of horse blankets and made myself a bed in the straw. I was actually pretty comfortable."

Ruth laughed at the image and Dillon silently groaned. Bill could go on forever so Dillon decided it was time for bed for him too. He stood up and started to the bedroom.

From the bedroom, Jill heard the thud of what she thought was a body hitting the floor. What was going on? she wondered as she left the bedroom. She almost fell over Dillon, who was sprawled on the floor.

"What happened?" Jill asked as Dillon turned over to

sit up. She looked from Dillon to Bill and Ruth. They were standing still, as if in shock.

"I tripped," Dillon replied. "On a floorboard." He got on his hands and knees to examine the faulty board. Bill came over and knelt beside him.

"It looks loose," Bill observed. "Actually, it looks like there are three or four loose." He wiggled them. "It looks like a trap door."

Jill joined the men on the floor. "It does look like they are there for a reason," she said. "Do you think there's something under there?"

Ruth gave a squeal of delight. "Maybe it's treasure," she suggested. "A buried treasure."

Jill doubted that, but gave permission for the men to lift out the board. Dillon used the flashlight on his phone to look inside.

"There's something in there," Bill said. "Pull it out, Dillon."

Chapter 9

Dillon was not pulling anything out of a hole in a floor in an old cabin. It could be an animal, or worse, a dead animal. He pulled the adjoining boards away.

"You do the honors, Bill," Dillon said. "I'll hold the light."

Bill reached in and pulled out a metal container. "I think it's an old coffee can," he said, holding it up for everyone to see before he gave it to Jill. "It has a metal lid."

Jill carried the can over to the table. The other three followed her and they all sat down. Jill examined the can. She could barely make out words on its sides.

"Definitely coffee," Bill announced, "but really old. Are you going to open it?"

Jill wasn't sure she wanted to. She looked at Dillon.

"I'm not opening it," he said, putting his hands in the air.

Jill handed the can to Bill. "You do the honors, Bill."

Bill worked the rusty lid off and looked in. The other three glanced in and Dillon and Jill both breathed a sigh of relief when they realized there was nothing dead inside. Bill handed the can back to Jill.

She took the items out one at a time. There was a packet of old letters, a photo of a young woman and another of a young child as well as several silver coins, several newspaper clippings, a gold necklace with a locket hanging from it.

"These must be my great-grandfather's," Jill said. "I recognize the name on the envelopes, but I don't know what the rest of this is." She held up a newspaper clipping and read. "This is a death notice for a woman named Elizabeth Perkins. I don't know who that is."

They all took a turn looking at the items. Dillon examined the coins and declared they were likely valuable. Bill looked at them and agreed. Jill was puzzled about the find. It was clear they were all from the 1920s or 1930s. She put them all back in the can and closed the lid.

"Seems like you've got a mystery on your hands," Bill said, rising from the table.

It was interesting, Jill thought, but hardly a mystery. She would take the can to her parents and they could look at what was inside. They likely knew the story of the items in the can. Still, it was kind of fun to find.

Bill went back over to the hole in the floor. "I wonder if there's anything else in here," he said and felt around with his hand, but there was nothing there. He picked up the floorboards they had removed and he and Dillon made quick work of repairing the floor. As everyone headed to bed, Dillon wished he could spend the night with Jill. He sighed and met Jill's glance.

She smiled and blew him a kiss. Dillon took it as a promise for another day. Hopefully, it would quit raining soon.

****

The next morning, the storms had passed and the sun was coming up over the trees behind the cabin.

Dillon woke to the smell of coffee brewing. He thought about last night's events. He wasn't wild about the extra company, but spending the day and then the evening with his mother and Bill had brought out a new appreciation for the older man. He was attentive and kind to Ruth and patient with Penny, respectful to Jill. Bill was still a little wary of him, Dillon could tell, but that was probably warranted. He vowed to make that right.

Jill also smelled the coffee and when Penny bounced onto

the bed, she decided it was time to get up. Ruth was already up and about, and to Jill's surprise, she and Bill were busy making pancakes when Jill got to the kitchen. A plate of bacon was sitting on the stove.

"Good morning, everyone," Ruth greeted them as Dillon followed behind Jill and Penny. "We want to get an early start this morning so we thought we would get breakfast started."

Bill nodded as he flipped a pancake.

A few minutes later, everyone was sitting at the table discussing last night's storm.

"Boy, I'd like to stay and do some more fishing," Bill said, "but I've got some things to do at home to get ready for tomorrow's memorial service."

"You are welcome to come back anytime," Jill said. "Just check with me for open dates and it's all yours."

Once breakfast was over, Jill and Dillon helped them finish loading Bill's pickup. Dillon pulled Bill to the side and offered his hand. "Thanks for coming," Dillon said. "I'm glad you brought Mom out here."

Bill, clearly surprised, shook Dillon's hand. He nodded and turned to help Ruth into the pickup.

"Alone at last," Dillon said as they drove away. He stood behind Jill with his arms around her waist.

"Not quite." Jill laughed as Penny raced to them.

"Can we go fishin' again?" she asked. "I love fishin.'"

Dillon looked at her and started to respond but Jill interrupted.

"Why don't we go look for some of those rocks you wanted to find?' she asked her daughter.

"Yes!" Penny shouted and ran to the lake's shore where she slowed to intently look for special rocks.

The morning passed pleasantly and after lunch Dillon

suggested an outing.

"Why don't we do a little more exploring?" he asked. "I noticed a couple of paths winding around here."

Penny was off the porch before Dillon stopped talking.

Dillon hoped there would be a little privacy as well. If he had to go many more minutes without giving in and touching Jill, he was going to be a basket case. Being this close to her and having to act casually, like they were just friends yesterday, had driven him to distraction. As they started to walk, he caught the subtle scent of her and immediately wanted to take her back to the cabin.

The outfit she was wearing didn't help matters, he thought a few moments later as he escorted her along the path. It was a jumpsuit thing that from the front looked very demure, but left Jill's legs and back bare, and sent Dillon's temperature up about ten degrees when he put his hand on her back to guide her around a boulder.

"So, tell me about your parents," he said conversationally, trying to keep his mind off of her bare skin so he wouldn't ravage her right there in front of Penny. "Do they live in Minneapolis?"

"Yes," Jill answered, trying to keep her mind on the conversation. As much as she liked having Dillon close, the pressure of his hand against her bare back was disturbing to say the least. The outfit seemed like a good idea back in her bedroom, cool and comfortable, but now she changed her mind. "That's where we grew up. My dad is a surgeon and my mom works at the hospital as a dietitian. That way, even with Dad's odd hours, they get to see each other."

"And your brother? Is he younger than you?"

"No, he's the oldest," she said, as the two fell into an easy gait with Penny running ahead and then coming back to them every few minutes. "He's a meteorologist."

"A weather man?"

"Yes, for KMNN in Minneapolis. Ever watch it?"

"Um, I don't recall seeing him, I generally stick to the Mankato stations for news and weather," Dillon admitted.

"Then there's Jan. She's exactly a year older than I am."

"What do you mean, exactly? You have the same birthday?" That was difficult to believe.

Jill nodded. "So do Peggy and Penny, except they were born the same year."

"Eerie. And they look exactly alike."

"My mom says it runs in the family," Jill said, smiling. At least Dillon believed her, many people didn't when they learned about the birthdays. "She and one of her brothers have the same birthday, and I think it continues back like that for several generations."

"That's really amazing, when you stop to think about it," Dillon mused, almost to himself. "I wonder what the odds for that are."

Jill shrugged. She wondered what the odds were that she could get Dillon to kiss her in the next thirty seconds. Unaware that she had done so, Jill slowed her walk, forcing Dillon to do the same.

As they rounded a bend in a path, they came upon a boulder shaded by a clump of pine trees. Dillon moved toward it and sat, drawing Jill with him. She looked around. They were on the bluff overlooking the lake and she could see the water below, glimmering in the sunlight. James Lake was like most of the state's lakes, left by massive glaciers thousands of years ago as the ice masses moved slowly back to the north, leaving the craters that formed the lakes and millions of boulders like the one on which they were sitting. It was one of her favorite spots here, but more importantly at the moment, they were mostly alone. Penny was playing with a stick, stirring the water in a puddle formed by last night's rain.

Jill sighed with longing as Dillon touched her lips with his, gently at first, but becoming more demanding, more intimate as Jill's mouth opened to him, causing a flame of desire to ignite within her.

He drew her closer as Jill moved her hands up and around his neck, feeling the silkiness of his hair. She loved doing it and was positive she would never grow tired of the feel of his hair. She could feel his hands caressing her bare back, sending delicious shivers up her spine.

Stop, they had to stop, Jill told herself. Penny was right there. One of Dillon's hands moved around to gently cup an unconfined breast through the material of her outfit, bringing the nipple to a tight bud. Jill moaned as Dillon lowered her to the boulder, its coolness deflecting some of the heat Dillon's hands had caused.

She could feel the hardness of his arousal against her leg, heard his own moan before he gently released her lips. He smoothed several tendrils of hair away from her face as she looked up at him, her puzzlement evident. Why had he stopped?

"Penny." Dillon smiled gently as he answered her unasked question.

Penny was standing next to them with her hands on her hips. "You guys were kissing," she stated. "And I'm hungry."

Jill blushed and lowered her eyes as she was brought back to the present and noted their surroundings. Now that Dillon had stopped those toe-curling kisses, she could feel the hard planes of the boulder against her back. Still, one of his arms supported her and the other still caressed her breast. It was as if he couldn't resist.

"I see we're both still fully clothed, so that's something," she whispered so Penny couldn't hear. She looked into his eyes, those eyes she could lose her soul in. She could see the smile that curved his lips shine in his eyes.

"I could change that," he breathed with a hint of promise in his voice.

"I bet you could. But you're right, this isn't the place." Jill straightened and Dillon released her. She pulled a granola bar out of the backpack she carried and gave it to Penny. She perched on the boulder, drawing her knees up and clasping them with her arms. Dillon hefted Penny up beside her.

"You look so comfortable, like you've sat here a hundred times," Dillon said, assuming a similar position.

Comfortable? With the memories they made just minutes ago still causing her body to tremble with reaction? Comfortable? When what she really wanted was to strip Dillon's clothes off and make passionate love to him right here, rock or no rock? Penny or no Penny? Stop it, Baxter, before you do something reckless. She took a deep breath to steady her senses before she spoke.

"I think I have. I used to sit here for hours and hours when I was little, dreaming about the world. I always wondered what was over that ridge," Jill said, pointing across the lake. "I always wondered if it was where my world ended and another began, one filled with castles and knights and unicorns. I dreamed that as I sat on this rock, a man, a knight, came riding over the ridge and whisked me away to his castle where I became queen, with nothing to worry about except what beautiful dress and jewels I would wear that day." She smiled wryly. "I guess they were teenage dreams, something to help forget about school and things like boys, or a pimple popping out on my nose right before a big dance."

Dillon sat mesmerized, as much by her words as by the sensual tone of her voice as she spoke. His Jill was a dreamer! He had never pictured her as a dreamer and was sure that it wasn't a side she let many people see. Of course, he shouldn't be surprised, since he knew her passion in his arms, but she usually showed a more practical side, and seemed content with her life. Could it be that Jill wasn't quite as content as she appeared? Could it be that she really dreamed about getting married again? He remembered the first time they met, when Jill said she wasn't interested in him, but look how that had changed. Even he had changed his mind and now he wondered if she could have changed her mind as well. But why hadn't she said anything? He would have liked to pursue that thought, but Jill was speaking again.

"I promised myself that someday I would climb that ridge."

"And did you?" Dillon asked in a hushed voice, almost afraid of her answer.

Jill shook her head. "No. I decided if the castles weren't there, I didn't want to know. Now that I'm older I can guess what's there and it's probably just another corn field." Her voice faded out as she closed her eyes, remembering her dreams. And thought about all the times she had sat on the very boulder and dreamed about her knight, her dream knight, riding a white horse and scooping her up and into his arms. They would ride off together, over that ridge and he would kiss her tenderly, then passionately, before laying her in a bed of flowers and making sweet love to her.

None of those fantasies had come close to the reality of Dillon kissing her, touching her, making her feel wanted. Like a woman. And it had been a long time. Sometimes Jill wished she was still that teenager and could still dream about a fantasy world near enough to reach and capture in her hand.

Dillon was relieved as they sat in comfortable silence with Penny between them, but he wasn't sure why. He wondered what Jill dreamed about now, as an adult. He knew it couldn't have been easy for her after her husband left, but she was incredible woman, as he was learning every day. She always kept her sense of humor and managed to stay calm, even in situations like last night.

"How do you do it?"

Dillon wasn't aware he had spoken aloud until Jill opened her eyes and turned to him.

"It's easy. I just sit here and close my eyes. It's peaceful."

"And quiet," Dillon added. "Too bad we don't have a bathtub."

Jill raised an eyebrow but didn't comment. She knew what he meant, but didn't trust herself to speak. It was too bad they didn't have a bathtub.

"But that's not what I was talking about," Dillon continued, noting her silence. "I just wondered how you manage to stay so calm and cool all the time, like the other night. You took control while all I did was blither like an idiot."

"It's something you learn as a parent," Jill said, understanding he wasn't joking. "After a while very few things surprise you, and even those generally have a humorous side. Once when Penny was a toddler, she managed to sniff a chocolate candy up her nose. I called the doctor in a panic only to have him tell me it would eventually melt." She smiled at the memory. It was messy, but it did melt.

"You have to admit, the last couple of days have been pretty interesting," she added. "You know you accused your own mother of lurking in the bushes?"

At Jill's laugh, Dillon joined in with a chuckle of his own. She was right. He had been caught off guard, had expected his mother to be where she always was, at home. And when she backed out of the bushes just after they had discussed that very possibility, he had been startled. Startled? He had been more than startled, he had been scared silly. And he had acted silly. He joined Jill's laughter, finally seeing the humorous side of the whole incident.

When they finally wiped the tears from their eyes and their laughter diminished to the odd chuckle, Dillon reached over and kissed Jill with a big, smacking kiss. He finally realized what drew him to Jill. Sure, she was beautiful and there was the physical attraction, but she made him angry and she made him want to protect her. She exasperated him and she made him laugh. She made him feel, something he never realized he wasn't doing. And it was great, absolutely great.

"What was that for?' she asked in surprise, looking at him and noting the grin on his face and the sparkle of laughter in his eyes.

"For being you." He slid off the rock and pulled Jill to her feet.

"I couldn't believe my mother went fishing yesterday," he added. "I don't think she's ever done that. My dad was a city guy and while he liked sports, he didn't do things like fishing and hunting." He helped Penny off the rock.

Jill let herself be pulled along the path, wondering about the change in Dillon. What had she said now? All those men who said they didn't understand women had never been around Dillon Hanley. If she lived to be eighty, Jill still wouldn't understand men. She didn't understand her ex-husband or her brother and now Dillon. All of a sudden he was happy and she had no idea why.

Dillon's good mood continued the rest of the day. He sat on the beach and played in the sand with Penny. He built a stone fort with her and as the sun set across the lake, sat between the little girl and her mother and thought, he had it all, right there, right then. He was absolutely, positively in love with Jill Baxter.

****

"I've never seen my son this happy," Ruth observed as she and Jill sat in Jill's kitchen on a Friday afternoon three weeks later, podding peas from Jill's garden. Ruth had finally gotten permission to take off her brace and she could perform regular tasks again, even something as small as podding peas.

Penny sat at the table with them, trying to help, although both women suspected she was eating more of the peas than she was putting in the bowl. It was a gray day, perfect for the job they were doing and giving them a chance to visit. Rain that week had kept everyone indoors for the most part. Dillon had been out of town for part of the week and Jill had been gone last night when he had stopped by to check on Ruth.

"I would like to think that I've caused the change in him," Ruth said, her eyes sparkling, "but I know you're responsible. You're good for him Jill."

"I don't know about that," Jill replied. "I don't know exactly what happened that Sunday, but all of a sudden there was a change in him."

"He apologized the other night for the way he's treated Bill," Ruth said, "and particularly for the night of the bush lurking." She laughed. "I don't think I'll ever forget that. But never mind, what I wanted to say was that Dillon has always been pretty sober. Until he met you, that is. Sure, he dated and entertained clients and such but I don't think I've ever seen him go into it with much pleasure. I don't think he would go to the circus for just anyone, even an important client."

"Don't forget, he was roped into that," Jill said. "I'm flattered but I suspect it might have more to do with Penny than myself."

"He does seem to adore her." Ruth reflected for a moment. "That in itself says something."

"What?"

"He's never shown any interest in children, even Jason and Meredith's little Ben. Now," she ruffled Penny's hair, "this pretty little girl seems to have stolen my son's heart."

"I didn't steal anything," Penny piped in, just now turning her attention to the conversation. "Mommy told me stealing isn't nice."

"Your mother is right," Ruth told Penny as she sorted out more peas. "I've seen a change in Jason too," she added.

"What kind of change?" Jill asked.

"I don't think you've met him, have you dear?" As Jill shook her head, the older woman continued. "He's called every day just to see how I am. He even talked about coming to visit tomorrow, but I convinced him to keep his golf date with Dillon and come over on Sunday instead."

Jill was silent, wishing she could find a way to steal Dillon's heart. She thought her plan would work, that by making love to her, he would discover deeper feelings for her. So far there wasn't any evidence of that. They had that one night, but hadn't been together since then. Maybe it wasn't as good as she thought. She thought sleeping with him would be enough, that sex would be enough, that she could live with those terms. She finally admitted she wasn't content seeing him every now and then. It didn't matter that he called her every night. The soft, sensual tone of his voice promised so much, but promise was nothing when she had to sleep alone every night.

She sighed. More time, she just needed more time alone with him. But there was no point in worrying about it right now. Jill turned her attention back to her task and her daughter as she chatted with Ruth.

She was telling the older woman about her upcoming trip to see her grandparents in Minneapolis, how she and Peggy were going to spend a whole week there and would get to go to the zoo and lots of other things.

That was it!

Penny would be gone for a whole week. She and Dillon would have time to spend together. If he wanted to, Jill thought, and she wasn't sure he did.

Suddenly Jill was tired of sitting and cleaning peas. She wanted to jump and shout. It may not be a good plan, she thought, but it was something.

Just then, the doorbell rang. By the time Jill excused herself, Penny had raced to the front door. She entered the living room just as Penny opened the door to admit the very person she wanted to see. Dillon. She stopped as he came into the room. He lifted Penny to hug her and their eyes met over her shoulder. He strode to where Jill was standing.

"Hello," he said, brushing his lips across hers. He realized he shouldn't be kissing her mother in front of Penny but he couldn't help it. As it was, he not only wanted to kiss her, he wanted to take her to the bedroom, take her clothes off and make long, passionate love. "I have a surprise for the two of you," he said instead.

"For me?' Penny asked. "Where is it? Can I see it?" She

squirmed down from her perch and ran to the front door to look.

Jill saw the desire flash in Dillon's eyes as he released Penny. It was gone in a second as Ruth stepped into the room.

"I thought I recognized that voice," she said, smiling.

"You haven't moved in here, have you?" Dillon asked with a teasing smile of his own as he gave his mother a hug and a kiss on her cheek.

"I've considered it," she answered. "Short of that, I've thought about putting a gate in the fence so I don't have to walk all the way around on the front sidewalk. But never mind, did I hear someone say surprise?'

"Dillon says he has a surprise for us, Grandma Ruth," Penny shouted, racing back to the adults. "Can we see it, can we?"

Jill and Ruth both looked at him expectantly as Penny bounced up and down. Dillon was suddenly afraid they wouldn't be as pleased with his surprise as he was.

"Well, it's not a surprise that you can see," he told Penny hesitantly. "I just decided I want to spend extra time with the two of you, so I'm taking next week off. We can do all sorts of things together."

He look at Jill to see her reaction as Penny jumped up and down even faster and his heart almost stopped. What was that he saw in Jill's eyes?

"That sounds wonderful," she said huskily. She hadn't thought they would be able to spend their days as well as their nights together.

Ruth caught the look they exchanged and smiled. She remembered cautioning Jill about Dillon but she saw a change in him. They didn't need her around, so maybe this was the perfect time to make some plans of her own. Bill had asked her to travel with him to Canada to visit his daughter, but she had been afraid neither of the boys would allow it. Now it was likely that at least one of them might not notice if she was gone.

Peggy stopped jumping and was looking at her mother with a solemn expression.

"Isn't next week when I'm goin' to my other grandma's house?"

The question startled Jill. She hadn't made the connection. "Um, yes it is."

"Does that mean I don't get to go?" Penny asked.

Jill knelt down. "No, not at all. I guess it means you get to decide what you want to do."

There was silence in the room while each adult considered Penny and the decision she was going to have to make.

Dillon had just seen another opportunity open up. He adored Penny, but the chance to spend time alone with Jill for an entire week conjured up images he hadn't dared dream about.

Jill loved her daughter and as much as she wanted the time alone with Dillon, she knew if their relationship was going anywhere, it was important for him to know that Penny came first.

Ruth thought how grown up this child appeared. Penny's decision made no difference to the older woman, but it almost brought tears to her eyes to watch the expressions on her face as she considered the question.

Finally Penny spoke. "Will Peggy still get to go to grandma's?"

"Yes, she will," Jill answered, wondering what her daughter was thinking. It wasn't long before she found out.

"Then I'm going too," she stated. "Where Peggy goes, I go.

Is that okay?" she asked in the next breath.

Dillon squatted down and brushed the hair back from Penny's face with his fingers. "You know it's okay with me, Penny. I want you to have fun at your grandmother's house, and you and I will have lots of time to spend together later."

And he hoped that was true, because he intended to convince Jill she couldn't live without him. He was going to show her that he loved her and that the only thing that would satisfy him was marriage. Hopefully, by the time Penny came home her mother would have agreed to marry him.

Chapter 10

His campaign actually didn't get started until Sunday night because he didn't go along to take the girls to Minneapolis. Instead, he kept his golf date with Jason on Saturday and spent Sunday with his mother.

"Do you know that I've seen you more in the last few weeks than I did in almost the whole previous year?" Ruth asked her son as he helped her wash her car Sunday afternoon. Dillon could easily have taken it to the car wash, but it was a beautiful day and this is what Ruth wanted to do.

Jason and Meredith had come over for lunch as well and Dillon couldn't remember when his mother had been this happy. Of course, neither Dillon nor Ruth had brought up the subject of Bill Weaver, knowing Jason would have to grill his mother about the man.

"And you're wondering what I'm up to, right?" Dillon said as he sprayed the hose on a soapy spot.

"Oh, I know what you're up to."

"And you're not going to say anything?"

"Oh heavens no. Well, maybe," she amended. "I just want you to be sure of what you're doing. I love that girl and I don't want to see her hurt."

"What about me? Aren't you afraid I'll get hurt?" Dillon asked, with a glimmer of teasing in his voice. He had no intention of hurting Jill, he loved her more than his mother could even imagine. Ruth rolled her eyes at him as if the matter even needed discussing.

"I guess I should feel lucky that Jill lives right next door. I have the feeling that if she lived across town, that's where you would be spending your time."

"You might be right," Dillon said seriously, "but I probably would have never met her if she didn't live next door to you. Thanks Mom."

"And you believe I wasn't matchmaking?" Ruth pushed her glasses up in confusion, finding it hard to believe herself that her son had just thanked her for introducing him to a woman. Oh, he had changed, she thought. It made her remember her husband, Alvin, who had swept her off her feet all those years ago.

"I believe it, and I'm sorry I ever accused you of trying to. And speaking of matchmaking, that little bit that Jill did for you worked nicely, didn't it?" he asked smugly, going around the front end of the car with the hose.

"Yes, it did," Ruth said, smiling dreamily. "And I wanted to talk to you about that."

"About what?"

"About Bill and I."

"You're not getting married, are you?" Dillon voiced his surprise. Maybe they should have talked to Jason.

Ruth threw her sponge at him, but Dillon easily ducked, grinning. It was part of the new Dillon Hanley. He had been stunned for a moment, but then realized that it really shouldn't matter if she was thinking about getting married, as long as she was happy.

"No, we're not getting married, although that's not a bad idea."

"So, you're going to live together."

"Now that's an idea too, but actually, Bill has invited me to go with him to visit his daughter in Canada," Ruth said cautiously. Dillon hadn't blown his top at the ideas of her getting married or living together, but they had been teasing. This was serious and whether she admitted it or not, she wanted his approval. "I know you don't like Bill very well, but he's a good man."

Dillon was silent for a moment, searching his mother's face, and then he came back around the car to put his arms around her. He hugged her, then drew back and held her at arm's length.

"I like him well enough and Mom, I love you. I want you to be happy and if Bill makes you happy, then I welcome him into our lives," he said quietly. "And if you want to go away with him, then he's a lucky man, because you're a very special lady."

"Oh Dillon," Ruth said, brushing away with the tears that formed at his words, "you're a very special man and I'm proud to have you as my son."

Suddenly uncomfortable with this unexpected closeness, Dillon blinked the moisture out of his own eyes, and releasing Ruth, bent down to pick up the hose again. He tried for a nonchalant tone when he spoke again.

"So, when are you running off to Canada?"

"Running off," Ruth puffed. "I am not… Oh you, you know I can't tell anymore when you're teasing," she said when she saw the grin reappear on his face. "As a matter of fact, we're leaving tomorrow."

"Tomorrow?" Dillon's eyebrows rose. "And you just now told me? Does Jason know?"

"Well, no, I thought maybe you could tell him."

"Sure, you want me to explain why I let our mother run off with a man he's never met."

Ruth laughed. "Yes, basically, that's it."

She squealed as he squirted her with the hose, causing Jill, who had just pulled up in the opposite driveway to wonder what had happened. Was that Dillon squirting his mother with a hose? It sure looked like him, and as he waved to her as she got out, Jill was sure of it.

Her heart beat faster as Dillon dropped the hose and crossed the grass in a sprint. He looked better every time Jill saw him, but she liked him the best in those tight jeans and that paint-spattered t-shirt. The only thing that would make him look better would be taking them off. Jill's cheeks burned as she realized the direction her thoughts were taking.

It was only a moment before Jill's face burned even more. Heedless of their audience, for Ruth had followed more slowly to welcome her back, Dillon gathered her into his arms and kissed her soundly. The world faded for her as Jill responded, drinking from his soft lips like they had been apart for weeks instead of two days.

Ruth cleared her throat. "Hello Jill," she said.

The couple broke apart to look at Ruth.

"Hello Ruth," Jill replied. "I'm back."

"I see that," Ruth replied. "You two have fun and I'll see you in a week or so." She walked back to her house. Neither of them saw her knowing smile.

Jill barely had time to grab her bag before Dillon whisked her off to his apartment.

"We're alone."

"At last." Dillon closed the door behind him, but didn't take his eyes off of the woman in front of him. He closed the small gap between them, claiming her lips with his own. It was a kiss similar to the one they had shared earlier, but it was completely different, Jill decided dreamily. The first one had been tempting, but this one, this one was the promise of things to come in only a few moments.

Jill ran her hands along the waistband of Dillon's jeans, letting them roam up under his shirt, touching and caressing the way she had wanted to outside her house. Here there was no audience and Jill could do what she had only fantasized. She pushed the soft garment up, and as Dillon obligingly lifted his arms, slid it over his head and let it drop to the floor. Now she was free to thread her fingers through the springy hair on his chest, where it swirled around his flat nipples. They hardened when she touched them. Dillon drew in his breath at the touch and once again claimed her mouth, demanding, and sending shivers of desire through her body, which arched instinctively, aching to be closer.

Her hands moved down to where the hair disappeared into the waistband of his jeans. A flick of her fingers opened the snap, and almost before he knew what had happened, Dillon was standing naked, allowing Jill's fingers access to his hardened arousal.

"Stop," Dillon moaned against her lips as he caught her hand, "or I'll take you here."

"There's no one to care," she assured him, and smiled serenely as he quickly undressed her, stopping only to smother one breast in kisses and then the other before he lowered her to the plush area rug on the floor, heedless of the hardness or the clothing strewn there.

"Oh, Jill I've missed you." He drew in a deep breath, striving for control, but Jill's hands could not be stilled as she caressed the muscles of his butt, loving the feel. He nudged her legs apart and entered her, making Jill gasp with pleasure. And then they moved together, as one, reacquainting their bodies in the most intimate way.

It was only when their world righted and their breathing was back to normal that they realized where they were.

"I'm sorry," Dillon groaned, and moved off Jill, but still cradling her softness with his arms.

"Sorry?" Of all of the things Jill thought he might say to

her at this point, that was probably the last.

"We didn't take any precautions, and I'm so sorry," he said. "I got a little carried away."

Jill breathed with relief. "It's all right," she said, looking into eyes filled with worry. "The time isn't right, but even if it were, this was my responsibility too."

It was Dillon's turn to be relieved. Although the thought of Jill growing with his baby made him ache with longing, this wasn't the time. He turned his attention to other things.

"I hate to say it, but I think I'm allergic to this rug," Dillon said, moving the shoulder that was resting on the rug. He was starting to itch.

"Don't tell me you've never..."

"I've never known a woman like you," he continued for her, "who put me under such a spell that I couldn't wait to get her alone." He stood, then pulled Jill up and into his arms before carrying her up the stairs to his bedroom. He set her down just long enough to pull back the blankets, then lifted her to curve against him again.

The sun was sitting low in the sky when a thought occurred to Dillon. He raised up from his comfortable position against Jill's shoulder where he had been dozing, to his elbow. He brushed the curls of hair away from her face.

She opened her sleepy eyes to smile at him.

"This is nice," she said softly.

He raised his eyebrows. "Nice? It's wonderful, fantastic and words I haven't even thought of yet. I love the thought of waking up to you every morning."

"Morning?" Jill was alert. "It's not morning, is it?" It was inconceivable that they could have slept the afternoon and entire night away, even though Jill felt rested and energized in a way she had never known.

"No, it's about dinner time," Dillon said, watching her stretch. "Aren't we expected to attend the barbecue tonight?"

"Barbecue?"

"At Jan and Grant's? Remember them?"

"Oh yes. I mean no," Jill said. "Jan and I decided that since we spent the weekend with our parents and both girls were away, we are going to dedicate the whole night to our men."

"I like the sound of that," Dillon growled, nibbling at her neck.

"But now that you mention it, I am hungry," Jill said, trying to ignore the delicious sensations he was creating with his mouth.

"Me too," was the muffled reply.

"For food," she laughed, pushing away from him and out of bed. "Do you have anything to eat around here?"

Dillon watched her stand, then look back at him when she realized she had no clothes. They were still in his car. He enjoyed her blush for a moment then also got out of bed and fetched her a shirt from his closet. He admitted though, that he preferred her just the way she was, a sweet distraction in the dim light.

"Thanks," Jill murmured, putting on the shirt. It was a little large for her, but just barely covered her hips.

Dillon decided the shirt was almost as tantalizing as her nudity. He could remember the curves and softness only hinted at now, remember how she felt in his arms.

He cleared his throat and headed to the adjoining bathroom, missing Jill's puzzled look. He wanted a shower but if he invited Jill they would never get anything to eat. He would probably also scare her to death if she realized how much he wanted her again, so soon.

"Why don't you go on down and I'll be there in a minute?" he suggested.

He couldn't be nervous, could he? Jill wondered as she went down the stairs. The sight of their clothes still strewn around caused Jill to stop for a moment, then she bent and quickly picked them all up and folded them in two piles. She drew Dillon's shirt to her and savored the smell that was uniquely his. She put it down and went into the downstairs bathroom to clean up.

She may not have said the words, and maybe she never would, but Jill loved him. Maybe she should consider marrying him, like he claimed he wanted. She was pretty sure he had fallen in love with Penny and would always treat her well. Maybe if they all lived together, he would come to love her too.

No, she couldn't do that. She made that mistake with Ron and he had said the words. But she had never felt so alive with Ron as she did with Dillon, so needed, so loved. She did feel loved by Dillon so maybe there was hope. He certainly cared for her.

She shook her head. This was getting her nowhere. Her stomach growled and she went to the kitchen. In the refrigerator, she found the ingredients for sandwiches and a bowl of potato salad. She was a little surprised that Dillon's kitchen was so well stocked.

Her thoughts went back to her dilemma as she moved to a stool and sat at the island to prepare sandwiches, stopping to munch on a piece of lettuce a moment later.

Dillon hadn't actually mentioned marriage again, so he was apparently satisfied with their relationship. Even happy about it. But why had he taken the week off to spend with her? Could it be that he wanted to be as sure as she was? It was so confusing. What if he asked her to marry him again?

Was it really important to hear those three little words to know how he felt? After all, she hadn't told Dillon that she loved him, but she did. And if it wasn't love Dillon felt for her, there was still something there.

She sighed, remembering their time together over the last few weeks. He was so demanding, but so gentle during their lovemaking. He could laugh at himself and with her and Penny, and share their fun. She suspected from conversations with Ruth he didn't do that much. Was that love? She thought so, but then she wasn't an expert. When she discussed it with Jan on their way back from their parents' house, Jan told her each relationship was different, but it certainly sounded and looked like love to her. It was that discussion that gave Jill the confidence to come here today.

She was glad she had, Jill decided as she watched Dillon approach. He was dressed in faded blue jeans that fit him like a second skin and the pale blue shirt he was wearing was unbuttoned with its tails hanging. He had seemed nervous upstairs, but the tension appeared to have evaporated with the water from his shower. He greeted her with a smile that melted her heart.

"I see you found everything," he said, helping himself to a soda from the refrigerator.

"I did," she said, laughing and handing him with a plate with a roast beef sandwich and some potato salad on it. "What did you do, stock up so we wouldn't have to leave your house all week?"

His guilty look made her laugh harder. "Well, I wanted to be prepared," he said, trying to look hurt and not laugh himself. She was just too sharp. He thought she must date men like him all the time and had figured out their little tricks. The thought sent a jab of jealousy through his stomach until he remembered their first kisses and how inexperienced she was.

"And I am tempted to keep you here all week," Dillon continued huskily, "but I suppose we should go out occasionally to get some fresh air."

"I hate to be practical but I will have to work part of the time," she said between bites. "I also need to weed my garden unless I can bribe your mother to do it."

"You'll have a hard time doing that," Dillon laughed. "She and Bill are leaving in the morning for Canada."

Jill paused in the middle of raising a forkful of potato salad. "Did you say Canada?' she asked, watching Dillon's face. The fact that Ruth was going on a trip with Bill didn't surprise her since she had often talked about traveling, but the fact that Dillon apparently knew she was leaving the country, with Bill, and was acting nonchalant about it did.

"I got you, didn't I?" he asked triumphantly.

"You were kidding," she stated, breathing a sigh of relief though she wasn't sure why.

But Dillon was shaking his head. "Nope, I'm not kidding."

Jill considered this. "And you're not upset."

"Nope," he said. "Well, I was, but we talked about it. She wasn't upset that we're spending the week together and she's an adult, so why should I be upset about what she does?" He shrugged.

To his surprise, Jill jumped off her stool and threw her arms around his neck, hugging him tightly. Instinct led Dillon to put his hands on her rounded bottom, but he realized it was bare and dropped his hands before he decided she probably wouldn't mind. Didn't mind, although she had stepped back just far enough to look at him.

"What was that for?" he asked, unable to stop the question.

Because I love you.

"The hug was for... I don't know, you and Ruth, I guess." As much as she wanted to say the words, she couldn't. The truth was, she wasn't sure why she hugged him. All she knew was that Dillon had finally stopped looking at his mother as only his mother and was now seeing her as a person. For some reason, that was important to Jill.

Any more reasoning beyond that was impossible as Dillon pulled her back to him and caressed her bare legs. She stopped thinking completely when he bent his head to her breast and suckled its roundness through his shirt. Within minutes they were back in Dillon's bed, trying to appease this other hunger that fed the soul as well as the body.

Afterward, Jill fell into a deep sleep and though Dillon would have liked to do the same, he made a trip downstairs to straighten up the kitchen. He retrieved her clothes from his car and brought everything upstairs before he joined her. He pulled her to him and they slept as one through the night.

The week passed quickly, too quickly, Jill thought. They spent much of their time at Dillon's but Jill still had obligations to her clients and had to check reservations for the homes being rented for a few days. She also needed to weed and water her garden. They watered Ruth's lawn and collected her mail as well. One day they drove out to the state park and walked to the waterfall. They strolled downtown and spent a couple of hours swimming in Dillon's pool.

On Friday, he surprised Jill by taking her to the local home improvement store. He wouldn't tell her why he was buying wood planks, even when he loaded them into his pickup. To Jill's surprise, they took everything to her house, where a carpenter was waiting.

Three hours later, Jill sat in a lawn chair and watched Dillon paint the newly constructed gate so that it matched the fence that separated her yard from Ruth's. She couldn't believe he hired someone to build a gate for his mother, but she was impressed. Jill tried to find out what had made him think of building the gate, but all Dillon would do was shrug and say he was tired of having to jump over the fence. Jill had never actually seen him jump over the fence, but she knew what he meant. Walking to the front sidewalk and around to Ruth's did get tiresome.

Not once did he mention playing golf, even on Saturday.

It had turned stormy that morning so they found a couple of old movies on his streaming service and spent most of the day watching them and munching on popcorn, in between making love there on the floor.

Because of an awkward rash on his shoulder from the first time they had used that part of the floor, they made a cozy nest of blankets and pillows in front of the sofa.

That's where they were when late in the afternoon, Jason called Dillon to invite him to dinner, and extended the invitation to Jill when he learned they were spending the evening together. Jill nodded her assent while Dillon was still talking, then went back to the movie. Dillon assured her it wouldn't matter if he missed a few minutes.

"Whoops," he said, bumping his palm against his forehead as he hung up the phone.

"Whoops? What kind of word is that for a banker to use?" Jill asked from her seat on the floor.

"That's a word we use when we forget to tell our brother important things, like why our mother hasn't returned any of his calls this week."

"Whoops," Jill replied. "Doesn't he know where she's at?

She said we wouldn't be able to reach her, there is very little cell service where Bill's daughter lives."

"Um, I didn't tell him and apparently Mom didn't either," he said, coming back to sit on the floor with her.

"So why didn't you tell him when you were talking to him and get it over with?" Jill asked. "Maybe you should text him now. He's not going to be happy that no one told him she's traveling."

Dillon grinned. "This is a moment to be savored," he said. "Jason thinks Mom tells him every little thing she does, just like I used to think. I think he should be sitting down when I tell him."

"You think it's going to be that bad?"

"Let's just say Jason's not as easygoing as I am," he said, reaching for her. When the powerful kiss ended, Jill drew a steadying breath. There was still one question on her mind and she wasn't going to be distracted.

"When are we having dinner with them?"

"In about..." he glanced at the clock sitting on the fireplace under the television, "two hours."

"Two hours?" Jill pushed away from him. "I need a shower. And what am I going to wear?"

"Relax, Jill," Dillon replied. "It's just my brother, not my mother."

Jill reminded herself of just that two hours later, as they walked up the stone sidewalk to the house where Dillon had grown up. Jason was just his brother, Jill told herself. Dillon had already told her he met Jan the week before at the country club, so she should be prepared. It's not like this was a job interview, so why did it matter so much? Jill wondered.

Dillon didn't knock at the front door, instead he opened it and allowed Jill to enter.

"Hello, Jason, Meredith, we're here," he called, causing Jill's eyebrows to raise. She thought her family was the only one that didn't stand on ceremony and made themselves at home at each other's houses.

"Dillon," greeted a lovely woman who was walking toward them from the back part of the home. Although the furniture was new, it reminded Jill of Ruth. The light airiness of the foyer continued into the living room where Meredith guided them. "And you must be Jill. I'm Meredith. I'm glad you could come, although I hear Jason forgot to issue the invitation until this afternoon."

Meredith saw the resemblance to Jan Humphrey, but she also saw the subtle differences in the way they carried themselves.

"It was no problem," Jill said, smiling. She generally trusted her first instincts and knew she was making a new friend. It really was no problem, she thought. They simply saved the last movie and the rest of the popcorn for later. Getting ready had taken some time since Dillon had insisted they conserve water and shower together. Jill wasn't sure they actually had conserved any water, and her cheeks reddened as she recalled the sensuous feeling of body against soapy body.

Just then Jill met Dillon's glance and her cheeks burned even more when she realized he was watching her and grinning, no doubt also remembering their intimacy.

Dillon turned to Meredith and was making the introductions as Jason came into the room, carrying his toddler son. He stopped still when he saw Jill.

"You're not... Jan Humphrey?" He remembered Dillon saying his lady looked similar to that real estate agent, but they couldn't look this much alike.

Jill and Dillon exchanged a smile before Dillon spoke.

"This is Jan's sister, Jill Baxter," he explained. "Jill, my brother Jason, and my nephew Ben."

"Twins?" Jason unknowingly echoed Dillon's first question to Jill. However, this time when Jill explained, Jason listened to the answer instead of leering at her the way Dillon had.

"No, we're not twins," Jill said, cooing to Ben as she did. "Jan's a year older than me."

Jason had the grace to close his mouth, even though he continued to stare at her.

It was strange, Jill thought, having Jason stare at her was not near as disconcerting as when Dillon had done the same thing. But then, Jason wasn't Dillon.

"When you and Susanne said they looked alike, I wasn't expecting mirror images," Jason said when he could speak again.

"Suzanne?" Jill picked up on the name, wondering idly if it was the same Suzanne she knew. No, it couldn't be. Granted, she didn't know much about Suzanne, but she was a quiet woman and didn't seem the type to frequent the country club.

"She does accounting for you, according to your sister," Jason continued innocently, "and is Dillon's regular golfing partner. Isn't it a small world?"

Golfing partner?

Dillon saw the surprised look on Jill's face. He knew it, he was dead. He cleared his throat, wondering how to get out of this situation, but Meredith broke into the conversation to say she needed to check on dinner. She suggested Jill keep her company and the women left the men, Meredith warning them to keep an eye on Ben.

Jill sent one last glance at Dillon as she left the room, silently promising this would be discussed later.

"So, you know Suzanne Hall also?" Meredith asked as she moved around the kitchen. The subject wasn't going away, but maybe she could diffuse it a bit.

"Yes, but I never would have guessed that Dillon knew her." No wonder he got nervous every time she mentioned blondes. He likely knew Jill and Suzanne were acquainted.

"Dillon's been a good friend to her," Meredith said. "They met in college. Suzanne was working three jobs and trying to keep her grades up. Dillon convinced his father to hire her at the bank for the summer and they became close. We thought they were going to get married at one time, but," she shrugged her shoulders, "that was several years ago and nothing ever came of it. I think they've just been waiting to meet someone else."

Jill digested this information and let out a sigh of relief. She didn't think Meredith would lie to her, and deep down, she wanted to believe Dillon and Suzanne were just friends. But she was a beautiful woman, and had a wonderful personality, everything a man could want. She chewed on her lip.

"Don't worry about it," Meredith said gently, noting Jill's expression. "It's clear Dillon's in love with you."

Jill jerked her head around, startled by the other woman's words.

"It's true," Meredith said, smiling. "And I bet he's in the other room reading Jason the riot act for bringing up the whole subject of Suzanne."

Jill was silent, thinking it over. When she realized Meredith was waiting for her to say something, she pushed the subject to the back of her mind. She wanted the evening to go smoothly where she was concerned, if only for Meredith's sake. None of this was her fault and she liked Meredith. The evening was already likely to have another bump in it.

"I think Jason is in for a little surprise of his own tonight," Jill said, smiling. She silently hoped Dillon would explain about his mother another time, but that wasn't likely to happen. Dillon's brother reminded Jill of him when she first met Dillon and she had a sneaking suspicion that Jason would not be happy when told of his mother's sudden and unexpected trip to Canada.

Meredith was another story, Jill discovered a few moments later. She had a sense of humor, that was evident. She laughed as she told Jill about Jason when they first brought Ben home from the hospital. According to Meredith, Jason thought babies were just little dolls, you put them somewhere and came back when it was convenient. It had taken several months for him to realize just what was involved with having a baby.

As she checked on the chicken, Meredith talked about how much Dillon had loosened up in the past few weeks, even interacting and playing with Ben more than he ever had before. Jason was very much like Dillon used to be.

"Although he is not near as stuffy as he was when we first met," Meredith laughed, straightening up from the oven. "But since his mother moved into the smaller house and we moved in here, Jason hasn't seen her as much as before. She doesn't want to come here because of the memories, and I can't say I blame her, even though I've tried to keep things pretty much the same."

"I think this is a wonderful house," Jill said, glancing around the large but cozy kitchen, "but I can see it might hold some painful memories for her. I think this house feels like it's been full of family who love each other."

"I do wish Ruth could have come tonight," Meredith

said, offering Jill a glass of wine. "We just don't see her often enough. Is it true she's seeing someone?"

Jill was saved from any explanation by the oven timer signaling the chicken was done. The subject wasn't brought up again until they midway through their meal.

"So, I guess you weren't able to get in touch with Mother either," Jason commented, causing Jill and Dillon to exchange looks, Dillon's amusing and Jill's slightly accusing.

"I didn't even try," Dillon said calmly, putting down his fork. "Canada's too far away to get here with only a couple hours notice."

His words had an immediate effect. Jason's mouth dropped open for the second time that evening. Meredith raised her eyebrows at Jill.

"Canada?" Jason asked.

"Your mother is in Canada?" Meredith echoed, her eyes beginning to sparkle as she caught Jill's slight smile.

"What is she doing in Canada?" Jason exploded, only to be silenced by Meredith's stern look.

"She left Monday to visit the daughter of a friend. She apparently didn't tell you?" Dillon asked. "I thought you knew until you said you had been calling her this afternoon."

"Right," Jason asked. "Who does she know with family in Canada?"

He was silent for a moment. "It's a man, isn't it?" Jason turned to glare at Jill and she had a feeling she knew what was coming. "I hear you're the one who introduced this man to our mother. And now she's run off with him."

"As a matter of fact, yes I did." Jill nodded. "His name is Bill Weaver..."

"I don't care what his name is," Jason got out between gritted teeth, "he's probably just a..."

"That's enough, Jason," Dillon broke in. He didn't like the direction this was going. "It's time we both realized that Mom is a grown woman and has the right to do what she wants with her life. We can't tell her what to do and what not to do."

"We should be glad for her," Meredith added. "I am happy she has someone to share her life."

"And fuss over," Dillon said.

"She has us to fuss over," Jason replied. "Maybe she could just find a few women to be friends with, it doesn't have to be a man. And now she's gone off to who knows where with a complete stranger."

"He's not a complete stranger," Dillon replied. "I've met him and spent some time with him myself. He's a pretty decent guy and makes her happy." He looked at the others at the table. "Maybe we should table this discussion for another time and enjoy our meal."

The subject was dropped but Jason was very quiet. He barely said anything and the evening passed uncomfortably. Even Ben was subdued by the mood.

Jill was disappointed, because she really thought she and Meredith could be friends.

Before she and Dillon left after dinner was over and Jill had helped Meredith clean up the kitchen, Meredith made arrangements with Jill to have lunch one day.

The silence between Jill and Dillon as they drove away was tense, despite the bright, moonlit night. The rain clouds had cleared away and left the night clean and cool, but neither occupant of Dillon's car noticed.

Here it comes, Dillon thought. She's got something to say about your relationship with Suzanne and she's going to say it.

Jill wasn't thinking about Suzanne, she was thinking about Jason and the rift she had caused between the two brothers by introducing Bill Weaver to their mother. She should have known how Jason was going to react. He reacted the same way Dillon did.

"I'm sorry."

Chapter 11

Their laughter broke the tension in the car as they both spoke at once.

"It was a fiasco," Jill said.

"It was uncomfortable," Dillon corrected. "I haven't seen Jason that upset for a long time. I bet he's still trying to figured out what happened. He's really too strait-laced."

"I don't think it was fair to blindside him like that," Jill said. "It was a conversation you should have had in private."

"I know, you're right," Dillon said. "But it was easier on everyone this way, trust me. I'm sorry he blamed you though."

"He should take a lesson from his brother," Jill said, laughing. "I hear he's not too serious about life."

"Not anymore." Dillon smiled and then lifted her hand to kiss it. "Thank you for that."

They rode in silence for a time, with only a few soft laughs lingering in the air. Dillon made his way to Jill's house. They had decided to stay there the last night since they weren't sure when Penny would be home. It was only as they lie entwined in her bed that Jill remembered Suzanne. She recalled the words Meredith said to her. He loves you. Did he?

"Dillon?"

His muffled reply from deep in his pillow made Jill smile. "Already? Again?"

"No," she laughed. "I was wondering when you were going to tell me about Suzanne Hall." It appeared he was closer to Suzanne than he was to her, Jill thought, figuratively speaking of course, as she felt Dillon's body tense.

He turned over and she could feel his shoulders shrug against her. "I probably know quite a few people you know too that we haven't realized. I didn't think it was important."

"You're right, it isn't," Jill replied.

"But it bothers you just the same," Dillon pointed out with accuracy.

"No. Yes, I guess it does. Suzanne means a lot to you, doesn't she?"

Dillon cupped her face with his hands. "She does mean a lot to me," he said gently but sincerely. "Suzanne has been a very good friend, probably the best friend I ever had until I met you. And she's been through some rough times so I'm glad I was a part of her life. Am a part of her life. But we were never in love."

Jill held her breath. Would he say it now? Would he tell her he loved her?

He didn't. Instead, he brushed a kiss on her lips. " Now, can we go to sleep? We need to be rested up for tomorrow."

"Tomorrow?" She asked as he effectively distracted her. "What are we doing tomorrow?" Tomorrow was Sunday and the Fourth of July, but Jill didn't recall making any plans other than going to Jan's for supper and fireworks. Her mind was still on the earlier discussion, what Dillon had said. Or rather, what he hadn't said. She wasn't really worried about Suzanne, she decided, although she admitted to just a tiny bit of jealousy when she thought of the closeness they shared. On the other hand, it was Jill who was lying next to Dillon tonight, not Suzanne.

"Dillon? Tomorrow?" she repeated when she realized he hadn't answered her question. There was no response except for the even breathing that indicated he was asleep. "Ohh, that's not fair," Jill muttered, punching her pillow. What was he planning? Penny would be home, she thought, and she missed her little girl so much. Being with Dillon was wonderful, but she would be glad to have Penny home. Not exciting, granted, so what else was he planning? Jill was afraid she wasn't going to get any sleep.

****

"Wake up sleepyhead."

Something was tickling her nose. "Mmph." Jill tried rubbing her nose on her shoulder but the feather-light touch continued. She opened one eye to look at Dillon, already showered and dressed. He was using several strands of her hair to tickle her again.

"Go away," Jill mumbled sleepily.

"It's Sunday," Dillon reminded her.

"So?"

"I have a surprise for you."

This time Jill opened both eyes. She was tempted to tell him to take his surprise and ... well, never mind. She had gotten some sleep last night, but not much, and unless Jill missed her guess, it was barely daylight.

Finally deciding she wasn't going to get any more sleep, Jill sat up and stretched. "Okay, Hanley, what's the surprise?" she asked impatiently.

He responded by pulling Jill from the bed and drinking in her sleepy beauty, unspoiled by clothes. He was tempted to forget about the whole day and take her back to bed, but settled for a long, leisurely kiss. They were both breathless when Dillon finally broke away.

"I know that's something that will never change," he said softly, holding her close.

"What's that?"

"When we're old and gray, I know that when we kiss, you'll still take my breath away," he replied.

She smiled and wondered sadly if they would still know

each other when they were old and gray.

He swatted her bare butt. "To the shower with you," he said. "I'll have breakfast ready when you're ready."

"How will I know what to wear if I don't know what the surprise is?" Jill asked, causing Dillon to turn at the door and look at her.

"It doesn't matter, whatever you choose will be fine," he said.

That was not much help, Jill decided. Someplace like the backyard or someplace like a fancy restaurant? She compromised by putting on blue jeans and a nice silky pullover blouse, but leaving her damp hair to curl around her shoulders. She knew the outfit would work no matter where they went. As long as they weren't going skydiving, she amended, as she went down to the kitchen.

"I think I'm overdressed," she muttered as she surveyed the scene. Instead of a cozy breakfast ready and sitting on the island, she found Dillon's bottom half jutting out from under her kitchen sink.

"Is this it?" Despite the fact that Jill thought his bottom half was adorable, she was a little disappointed.

"Is this what?" came the muffled reply.

"The surprise?"

Jill caught his frown as he scooted out and sat up on the floor facing her. "This is a surprise, not the surprise," he said, gesturing toward the sink.

She knelt beside him. "What happened?"

"I don't know. When I came down there was water running all over the floor. So far all I've done is turn off the water and mop up the floor. I think one of the pipes burst."

Now Jill knew why the water had suddenly gone off just as she finished her shower. It didn't really alarm her since she knew the city had been having trouble for the last couple of weeks with its pumping system and kept shutting the water off for short periods of time as they tried to make repairs.

Jill knew her pipes needed to be replaced, but she had put it off. She had already purchased new pipe but had other things on her mind lately. She sighed. She knew how she was spending at least part of her Sunday.

"You had better let me take a look," she said.

"I think we should call a plumber," Dillon said, moving aside.

"Be serious," was Jill's reply as she scooted under the sink for a look. "Do you know how hard it is to get a plumber on a Sunday morning?"

Dillon didn't answer. He was distracted by the attractive view of Jill's legs as she wiggled back out.

"Are you listening to me?" she asked as she took in his expression. It was the same one he used when he was thinking about getting her into his bed.

"What? Oh yeah, hard to get a plumber," he finally said. "I know a couple of them."

"Right. And they would be more than happy to come over here on a Sunday morning for a little leak." Jill straightened her blouse, wondering what was going on in his mind. "I'll be right back." She left the room before Dillon had a chance to say anything.

He looked around, running a hand through his hair. He wished he had started a pot of coffee before he went to wake Jill.

When she came back a few minutes later, Jill had exchanged her blouse for an old t-shirt and her heeled sandals for a pair of old tennis shoes. She was carrying a tool box. "Let's get to it," she said.

"We're not going to try and fix this ourselves, are we?"

Jill shrugged. "I don't know what other choice we have, unless your surprise was so important it can't wait," she said.

Dillon thought of the ring in his jacket pocket in the other room. He was dressed in jeans and a white shirt. He had wanted to ask Jill to marry him several times in the past week, but the timing was never right. Now, if he wanted to propose in private, he needed to do it before Penny got back. He thought maybe they could drive out to the waterfall but it looked like that would have to wait.

Maybe this plumbing thing wouldn't take long. Maybe the problem was minor and Jill knew what she was doing. Maybe he could help her, even if he didn't know the first thing about plumbing. Maybe he should sit down.

Jill was waiting for his answer.

"No, it can wait," he said. "Are you sure you want to do this?" Dillon indicated the sink. He had visions of the house floating away. He was sure that is what would happen if he was doing it.

"Trust me," Jill said. "Now, why don't you go get us some coffee and donuts while I get started here? I could use some caffeine and something to eat."

"Right," he replied. "Why don't I do that?" Dillon left the room shaking his head as Jill crawled back under the sink. His "have a good time" was followed by her "I will."

It was nothing short of miraculous, Dillon thought later as he turned on the kitchen faucet to wash his hands, then opened the cabinet door below. All new pipe and not a leak anywhere. He shouldn't be surprised, Dillon told himself as he wandered out the back door.

Jill could do anything she set her mind to. But plumbing. She had done a professional job, only laughing when he suggested she go into the plumbing business full time. Jill told him that as a home owner and property manager, it was to her advantage to be able to take care of some of the odd jobs around a house.

Now she had gone outside to cut some flowers and check on her garden. They expected Penny back any minute and Dillon's only regret was the small jeweler's box still resting in his jacket pocket. Plumbing and marriage proposals didn't go together.

Dillon was still contemplating when the time would be right when Penny bounded into the house, running to hug Dillon as he rose from the sofa to meet her. After a quick kiss on Dillon's cheek, she asked for her mother. He looked up to see a dark-haired man entering after her, wearing blue jeans and a shirt open at the neck. He also had the blackest hair Dillon had ever seen, pushed back from his forehead and a neatly trimmed mustache and short beard. Dillon would have died for the beard and mustache. Somehow his never grew in that thickly or evenly.

"She's out cutting flowers, but I bet she would love to see you," Dillon said as the youngster dashed through the kitchen and out the back door before he was finished speaking.

Shaking his head, Dillon turned to face the other man, whom he estimated to be about his same age.

"I'm Dillon Hanley," he said, offering his hand.

"Nance L'Breck." he introduced himself. "I'm... I'm a friend of Ron Baxter."

Ron Baxter? Jill's ex-husband? A friend?

"I see," Dillon said carefully, withdrawing his hand. "Come on over and have a seat. I'm sure Penny and Jill will be back in a minute."

Dillon went back to his place on the sofa and was surprised when the other man sat down next to him, nearer than Dillon thought was necessary. He moved over a bit. He cleared his throat and spoke, trying to ease the uncomfortable feeling he was getting. Something was wrong here.

"So. You brought Penny home." That fact bothered Dillon more than he wanted to admit. If Penny needed a ride home, he and Jill could have gone and gotten her. Jill said her parents called earlier and were bringing the girls back to Mankato. Instead of dropping Penny off at Jill's, they would all meet at Jan's for the weekly barbecue later that evening. Dillon hadn't given it much more thought. But then, he hadn't expected this. This friend of Jill's ex-husband was joining in on the day's festivities?

"Yeah," Nance said. "I was over at Jan's when Penny got there, so I offered to bring her home. She missed her mother." He moved a little closer to Dillon. "How long have you known Jill?"

"Um, a few weeks," he answered, trying to scoot unobtrusively to the far end of the sofa and away from this guy. What was he up to?

"Are you serious about her?" Nance asked the question as he moved closer to Dillon.

"Look," Dillon said, trying to stay calm. "I really don't think that's any of your business."

Nance shrugged and held up his hands. "Hey, it's no big deal. I just wondered if you were available."

"Available?" Dillon hoped he was misreading the situation.

"Yes," the other man answered. "I thought maybe you and I, we could go out, have a drink, maybe dinner?" An arm went around Dillon's shoulders.

Dillon's hopes were dashed. He jumped up from the sofa

and practically ran to the other side of the room. "Go out? Dinner?" he sputtered. "You and me?"

This was it, Dillon thought, he had officially entered the land of insanity. He thought he had regained some control over his life, but apparently not. What had happened to the nice, calm, sane life he had led up until a few weeks ago?

It had disappeared, that's what happened, Dillon decided and had been replaced with this... this, whatever this was. "Are you crazy?" he finally got out. "Who do you think I am?"

Nance shrugged. He calmly stood and nonchalantly put his hands in his pockets. "That's what I was trying to find out. But hey, it's no big deal."

"No big deal?" Dillon sputtered. "You waltz in here like you own the place, and... put moves on me and then you say it's no big deal? Buddy, if this wasn't Jill's house, I'd throw you out."

The other man didn't look scared. Okay, maybe he wouldn't actually throw him out. But he wanted to. "I ought to anyway," he said. He really just wanted the guy to leave.

"I want you to know I love Jill and I intend to marry her. I suggest you go." Dillon was practically shouting.

Jill had just opened the back door and heard the loud voices. She headed to the living room, Penny at her heels.

"What did you just say?" she asked Dillon, incredulous. Did he just say he loved her and wanted to marry her? "And why are you shouting at my brother?"

She turned her attention to Nance and gave him a quick hug. "Nance, hello, it's wonderful to see you," she said.

Dillon stood where he was. Brother? This guy was her brother? His eyes narrowed. What was that they just went through?

"You're Jill's brother?" he spit out. "Friend of her ex-husband?"

"What's going on here?" Jill asked the two men. She turned to her brother. "What have you done?"

"I was just trying to do you a favor," Nance said, glancing guiltily at Jill.

"By getting rid of him?" Jill nearly shouted.

"I just wanted to check him out, make sure he's not, well, you know, make sure he's right for you," he replied.

"What did you do?" she asked him.

"He asked me out." Dillon answered, struggling to lower his voice. "He just asked me out on a date. Your brother. I'm leaving now." He grabbed his jacket.

Jill watched in horror as the love of her life walked out her front door. She turned back to Nance.

"What were you trying to do?" she asked, nearly shouting herself. Remembering Penny and big ears, she squatted down. "Why don't you go outside and play while I talk to Uncle Nance?"

Jill directed her gaze back to her brother as the little girl ran out the front door to safer ground. She didn't know what was going on, but her mom was shouting and that was never good.

****

"Where ya' goin'?" Penny asked Dillon as he strode down the sidewalk.

"For a walk," Dillon ground out. He gentled his tone as he turned to watch the little girl try to catch up with him. "I just wanted to walk a little bit." The truth was, he couldn't storm off in his car, it was blocked in the driveway by what he assumed was Nance L'Breck's big SUV.

"Can I come?"

"What? Oh, sure," Dillon replied, looking down to see Penny running along beside him. He immediately shortened his stride so she could walk with him. He headed in the direction of Ruth's house.

She followed him up the walk to his mother's house.

"Grandma Ruth isn't home," Penny pointed out. "Mom said she went on vacation." She looked at Dillon expectantly as he lowered himself to the porch swing. Penny crawled up and sat beside him.

Dillon sighed. He didn't feel like talking, he wanted to … well, he wanted to slug that guy. He was pretty sure that wouldn't end well for him and Dillon wasn't a violent man. He needed to think. Jill's brother just introduced himself as a friend of her ex-husband. Did they stay in touch? Was there a chance he was coming back? Would he cause trouble for Jill and Penny, try to get custody of Penny?

Penny tugged on his sleeve.

"Do you know when she's coming back?' she asked. "I miss her."

"She should be back today, any time now,," Dillon answered, pulling his attention back to Penny. "And I miss her too."

They sat in silence for a few moments until Penny tugged on his shirt again.

"Are you mad at me?" she asked when he looked down at her.

Dillon answered immediately. "Of course not, Penny. Who could be angry at you?"

"My mom is," she said, tears forming in her big brown eyes. "She was yelling and told me to go outside and play. Do you think she wants me to go back to my grandma's house?"

"I'm sure she's not mad at you. I think she's angry at some-one else. She doesn't want you to go anywhere," he answered. "She's really happy you're home. Your mother loves you and so do I."

"I love you too," Penny said, planting a kiss on his cheek. Dillon forced his mind to stay focused on the little girl beside him who was trying not to cry. He gave her a hug and they were silent again.

"Are you going to marry my mom?"

Where did that come from? he wondered. He answered honestly. "I don't know."

"I hope you do. I need a dad," Penny said.

Dillon couldn't help the smile that formed on his lips. "You do?"

"Yeah, that's what my grandma said."

"Oh," was his only comment as he tried not to laugh aloud. For some reason it was comforting to know that even six-year-olds had people to manage their lives. But what Dillon wanted right now was more information on the uncle guy.

"Penny?"

"What?" she answered, looking up at him.

"Is Nance really your uncle?" There, he asked the question that was bothering him. The guy was a jerk. He couldn't imagine him being related to Jill and Jan.

"Uh huh." Penny nodded. "He's..."She screwed up her face as she thought. "He's my mom's brother. Yeah, that's it. And Aunt Jan is her sister. But Jan doesn't like to be called Aunt Jan," she confided.

Dillon breathed with relief, but only for a moment. If the man really was Jill's brother, why hadn't he introduced himself as her brother? Why had he said he was a friend of

Ron Baxter, and worse, why had he made that repulsive suggestion? Dillon was tempted to go back and tell Nance just exactly what he thought of him. He shook his head, trying to make sense of it, but only one thing was clear. Ron Baxter wasn't coming back and trying to claim Jill or Penny. Not if he had any say in it.

"Do you need a little girl?" Penny tugged on his shirt again.

"What? Oh, sure. Everybody needs a little girl."

"Can I be yours?"

Dillon's heart melted. He did need a little girl. He needed this little girl. And this little girl's mother. He would deal with Nance L'Breck, but maybe not today.

Dillon stood and pulled Penny up into his arms. "You sure can," he said. "Why don't we go ask your mom if that's okay?"

"All right!" Penny shouted and hugged him tight. He lifted her onto his shoulders and started down the walk.

Dillon knew that he was agreeing to becoming a parent as well as a husband and smiled. Why hadn't he thought of this before? Penny was his biggest ally. By committing to her, Jill would have to see how much he loved them both.

He fished the box out of his pocket and handed it up to Penny, giving her a few quick instructions.

Jill met them at the bottom step of her front porch. Nance was right behind her and regretting his earlier actions. It took a lot to get Jill angry, but when she did, watch out. He tried to leave, but Jill made him wait for Dillon to come back so he could apologize. Dillon had to come back, his car was still here. And Penny was with him.

Jill couldn't remember the last time she had been this angry. Never mind that Nance had been trying to be a good brother, he was out of line. He had probably chased Dillon off for good, so as he stopped to let Penny off his shoulders, she breathed a sigh of relief. A small sigh of relief since he was glaring at Nance.

Penny ran to her mother, obediently keeping one hand behind her back. Jill was watching him carefully as was the man standing on the porch.

Dillon followed slowly and stood behind Penny so he could see Jill's reaction when Penny started talking. He ignored the other man who was looking uncomfortable. He was not the confident man of a few minutes ago, Dillon thought. Jill had laid into him and he obviously was not sure what was happening. Dillon decided to let him sweat it out.

"Can I, Mommy? Can I, can I?" Penny jumped up and down.

Jill looked at Nance, then Dillon, but neither spoke. Nance merely shrugged his shoulders while the shadow of a smile played on Dillon's lips.

"Can you what?" Jill tried to focus on her daughter. Of all the scenes she had played through her mind, this wasn't one of them. At least Dillon hadn't just left. And he hadn't punched out Nance, which was what she wanted to do. He was waiting, Jill thought. But for what?

"Can I be Dillon's little girl?"

Jill's jerked her head up to look at Dillon. Dillon's little girl? What was she talking about? Dillon still didn't say anything, just smiled a little more.

"Uh, well... I suppose so..." she replied, keeping her eyes on Dillon.

"Yay!" Penny jumped up and down. "And you can be his big girl, right, Mommy?"

"What?" Jill was lost.

"And he can be my daddy," Penny continued. She jumped up and down and then hugged her mother tightly.

"Your daddy?" Who said anything about a daddy? All she had intended to do was set the record straight about Nance and his hare-brained ideas, and now Penny was talking about daddies?

"Yeah." Penny stepped back from her mother and presented the little box. "Here, this is for you."

Jill stared at the black velvet box, her heart pounding loudly.

"Open it Mommy. See," she said as Jill forced her fingers to move and snapped open the lid to reveal an exquisite diamond ring. "It's a 'gagement ring, right Dillon?"

Dillon moved over to the two loves of his life. "That's right," he answered, "and if your Mommy will let me put it on her finger, it'll mean we can be a family." He looked into Jill's eyes.

When he saw the tears gather there and the smile on her lips as she nodded, Dillon took the ring and sank to one knee. "I love you Jill," he pronounced. "Will you marry me?"

Her answer was a breathless "yes." Dillon slid the ring on her finger and rose as she vaulted into his arms, laughing and crying at the same time, causing Dillon to stagger backward before he regained his balance and kissed her thoroughly, heedless of their audience.

Penny continued to jump up and down as they kissed, while Nance decided that as touching as the scene was, it might be a good time to slip away unnoticed. He was wrong.

"I love you," Jill breathed as she settled into Dillon's embrace. A movement to her side made her stiffen and she straightened to face her brother.

"Not so fast," she warned.

Nance stopped in his tracks and slowly turned back. Two were glaring at him and the other was watching curiously. It was no use. He just hoped that someday they could all laugh about this. Nance decided to take the initiative.

"Congratulations," he said, offering his hand to Dillon. "You're a very lucky man. And I'm sorry about, you know, before."

Surprised, Dillon considered the bigger man, trying to judge his sincerity. What the hell, he could even like Bill Weaver right now. He put out his hand and they shook. "I don't know about lucky. Apparently, I'm getting you as a brother-in-law. But maybe I can try and forget about that," he said, looking lovingly at Jill and Penny before he turned back to Nance.

"Now why don't you get out of here?" His grin took the sting out of his words.

"Good idea," Nance replied. "I'm gone." He started down the steps.

"Penny, would you like to go back to Jan's with Nance and tell everyone your news?" Jill asked. "We'll be over in a little while." She gave the little girl a gentle push in the direction of her uncle.

"Yes!" Penny shouted, running to the car. "Dillon's goin' to be my daddy, Dillon's goin' to be my daddy."

Nance silently groaned, knowing what he was going to hear all the way across town. He turned back to Dillon and Jill and grinned. "Does this mean I'm off the hook?"

Dillon and Jill were looking at each other and smiling, lost in their own world. It was Dillon who finally spoke.

"Maybe," he said, "but if you ever pull a stunt like that again, you'll be eating your teeth for dinner."

Nance believed him. He looked like he would do anything for Jill, including taking him on. Nance preferred his teeth in his mouth. They were important for his job that entailed being in the public eye.

"I wouldn't even think it," he said, "but you take good care of my sister. I'll be watching."

Nance backed away as Jill advanced menacingly. He held his hands up. "I'm going, I'm going." He turned and walked to his vehicle as Penny started honking the horn.

A few moments later, as they drove away, Jill and Dillon burst into laughter. Penny was bouncing up and down in her car seat chanting, "Dillon's going to be my daddy!"

****

An hour or so later, Jill stirred from her comfortable position on Dillon's chest. After they finally controlled their laughter, Dillon scooped her up and carried Jill into the house and to her bed where they had sealed their commitment to one another.

Now that they had said the words, their love-making was even more special. As much as Jill wanted to stay in that moment forever, she knew her family was waiting for them at Jan's. She wanted her parents to meet Dillon. She also wanted to show off her ring. It was beautiful, as beautiful as the life promised by the gesture. To Jill, it meant spending the rest of her life with the man she loved.

"Dillon?"

"Hmm?"

"That was a sneaky thing to do," Jill said, "bringing Penny into your plan."

"I know, but it worked," he replied.

"It sure did," she acknowledged. "I think you made her the

happiest little girl in the world."

"I was hoping to make you the happiest girl in the world," Dillon said, stroking her hair.

"You've made me the happiest woman in the world." Jill emphasized the word 'woman.'

Dillon kissed her and his hands moved in hypnotizing circles on her thighs.

She sighed regretfully. "We should be going," Jill said, drawing little patterns in the hair on his chest.

"We are going," he said. He wanted to stay here and focus on those tantalizing fingers working their magic. Maybe no one would notice if they didn't show up.

Jill raised her head a fraction and looked at the familiar room. "I don't think so," she said. "We're still in bed."

He shifted so that their faces were inches from each other, sweetly distracted by the love he saw in her eyes. "We are," he said, "and I'm so happy we're going to share it for the rest of our lives."

"Umm," she agreed, meeting his lips. "Yes, we are."

They jumped apart as the front door banged.

"Yoo, hoo?"

It was Ruth. "Hello, Jill? Dillon? Anyone?"

Dillon groaned. Jill collapsed with laughter.

"Just a minute, Ruth," Jill shouted.

"It's my mother," Dillon announced unnecessarily as Jill jumped out of bed and grabbed a t-shirt and shorts. "What's she doing here?"

Jill didn't answer but suggested he get dressed as she darted out the door, closing it behind her.

"Ruth," Jill greeted the older woman and noticed Bill standing behind her. "You're home."

"Yes," Ruth replied. "I was looking for Dillon to let him

know I was home. I tried to call, but...."

Jill blushed. Dillon wandered out of the bedroom.

"Oh, there you are," Ruth greeted him. "Of course, well, don't worry about it," Ruth said. "We get it. We're going to head over to Jan's house. You two go back to what you were doing. We'll just be going." She grabbed Bill's arm and backed out the front door. "Don't mind us."

After Ruth and Bill left, Jill and Dillon took showers and dressed, then headed to Jan and Grant's house. Penny would never forgive them if they didn't come.

Jill introduced Dillon to her parents, Allen and Paula L'Breck. Dillon saw nothing of the parents in the two girls, but Allen and Nance looked very much alike, the handsome older man giving a glimpse of what Nance would eventually become.

The women oohed and ahhed over Jill's ring and Bill regaled everyone with stories from their trip to Canada.

"So, whatever happened with that old can we all found at the cabin?" Bill asked Jill as they feasted on steaks and an assortment of salads. There were chunks of watermelon and chocolate cake. In addition, Grant had helped the little girls make homemade ice cream that afternoon.

"I tried to make sense out of it," Jill said, "but it does seem to be a mystery. I gave it to mom so she could look at everything."

Paula L'Breck smiled. "I'm afraid I don't know much about it," she said, "but I'm not much of a mystery solver either, so I gave it to Nance. He's going to see what he can find out."

Everyone looked at Nance, who suddenly looked uncomfortable. He had tried to stay out of the way since returning from Jill's with Penny, not wanting to draw fire from the rest of the family. Thankfully, neither Jill nor Dillon brought up the earlier incident.

"I think it's interesting," he said to no one in particular. "I like history, so I'm going to see if I can put the pieces together." He turned to Jill. "I'll give it all back to you once I'm done since you're the one who found it."

"Technically, Dillon found it," Bill explained, laughing at the memory.

Since they had all heard the story several times already, everyone joined in the laughter.

Now, Jill sat back against Dillon's chest on a blanket on Jan's lawn and watched as Penny and Peggy twirled sparklers through the air. They both looked up as the first fireworks from below the bluffs lit up the sky, popping with color against the darkness. She sighed with contentment as Dillon leaned down to gently kiss her.

She was a distraction for sure, Dillon thought, but the sweetest one he could imagine.

About the Author

Although this is her first novel, Neesa Lee has been writing most of her life. She holds a BA in journalism from the University of Nebraska-Lincoln and spent years in the newspaper and print businesses. She has written everything from hard news to sports and a farm column, using those experiences to hone her writing style.

She is an avid reader and always enjoys a good story. She enjoys traveling and treats every trip she takes as a new adventure and new experience. Lee incorporates those expeirences into her writing, telling stories with unique characters that she would want to read.

Lee lives in Nebraska and owns her own antique store where she has the opportunity to meet and interact with a wide variety of people. She and her husband have three adult daughters, six grandchildren and three slightly spoiled dogs.

www.ingramcontent.com/pod-product-compliance
Lightning Source LLC
Chambersburg PA
CBHW070500200726
48293CB00007B/2309